Goosebumps
HorrorLand™

CREEP FROM
THE DEEP

ALL-NEW! ALL-TERRIFYING!

1. REVENGE OF THE LIVING DUMMY
2. CREEP FROM THE DEEP
3. MONSTER BLOOD FOR BREAKFAST!
4. THE SCREAM OF THE HAUNTED MASK

Goosebumps®

NOW WITH BONUS FEATURES!

NIGHT OF THE LIVING DUMMY

DEEP TROUBLE

MONSTER BLOOD

THE HAUNTED MASK

Goosebumps HorrorLand™

CREEP FROM THE DEEP

R.L. STINE

SCHOLASTIC

Scholastic Children's Books
A division of Scholastic Ltd
Euston House, 24 Eversholt Street
London, NW1 1DB, UK
Registered office: Westfield Road, Southam, Warwickshire, CV47 0RA
SCHOLASTIC, GOOSEBUMPS, GOOSEBUMPS HORRORLAND, and
associated logos
are trademarks and/or registered trademarks of Scholastic Inc.

First published in the US in 2008 by Scholastic Inc.
This edition published in the UK by Scholastic Ltd, 2008
Goosebumps series created by Parachute Press, Inc.

Copyright © 2008 by Scholastic Inc.
The right of R.L. Stine to be identified as the author of this work
has been asserted by him.

ISBN 978 1407 10694 6

British Library Cataloguing-in-Publication Data.
A CIP catalogue record for this book is available from the British Library

Printed and bound by CPI Group (UK) Ltd, Croydon, CR0 4YY
Papers used by Scholastic Children's Books are made from wood grown in

3 RIDES IN 1!

CREEP FROM THE DEEP

1

My name is William Deep, Jr. I'm from Baltimore, Maryland, and I live for adventure.

The people who think I'm a normal twelve-year-old call me Billy.

But the few who *really* know me call me by my *secret* name – the Undersea Mutant.

For me, danger is like breakfast. I can't start my day without a healthy, balanced bowl of *danger*.

Here I am in the middle of the ocean. Sure, it's dark and dangerous. But what do I call it?

Home.

I'm swimming off the island of Careebo, a tiny sand field in the Caribbean Sea. I peer straight ahead through my infrared snorkel mask. My laser-guided razor fins cut through the waves.

I follow a school of silvery angelfish, sparkling like diamonds in the sunlit waters. They don't seem to realize the danger nearby.

But my mutant senses are alert. No underwater villain can escape me.

You may remember some of my adventures.

I'm the one who defeated Sandy the Squid. He called himself the Cephalopod of Steel. Sandy liked to tickle swimmers to death – until I tied his tentacles in a knot.

Remember the Ragin' Ray of Honolulu Bay? He's not ragin' any more. How about Joe, the Great White Stingray? After a smackdown with the Undersea Mutant, he floundered off with his stinger between his fins!

The Snapping Tortoise of Terror? After our three-day underwater battle, I tossed him into a soup bowl. His new name was *Delicious*!

Yeah, I'm tough. But these are tough waters.

And now I'm about to face my most dangerous foe. The Albino Electric Eel. The only one in the known universe.

I see him waiting for me behind a bank of red and yellow coral. To *your* eyes, he's just a long string of seaweed. That's because you don't have Mutant Vision.

I lower my 4-D hi-def mask into the water and kick harder. I glide towards my foe. I don't hesitate. I grab him barehanded and begin to apply my famous Eel Squeeze.

ZZZZZZZZZZZZT!

Two hundred thousand volts of electricity shoot

through my body. Enough power to electrocute a dozen men. But to me, it's only a slight itch.

I thrash and kick, wrestling with this Eel of Evil. Another jolt of electricity makes the churning water start to boil.

Yes, it's getting hot down here. But the only one who's in *real* hot water is my wriggling enemy!

I hear a voice . . . a distant voice, calling my human name. "Billy? Billy?"

A desperate cry for help. Someone is in danger.

I let go of the eel. *Catch you later!* I think. I fight my way to the surface.

Someone needs me!

"Billy? Billy?"

I bobbed up to the surface, pulled off my snorkel, and raised the mask. I stared into the sunlight.

I saw my uncle. He was leaning over the rail of his boat, the *Cassandra*. He stared down at me.

"Billy? What are you doing down there?" he called.

"Uh . . . just pretending stuff," I said.

"Was that *seaweed* you were fighting?" he asked.

I didn't know he was watching. "I thought maybe it was an eel," I said.

He chuckled. "Well, you gave it a beating it won't forget!"

Dr D thinks my superhero fantasies are funny. "Climb up here," he shouted. "You've been pestering me for weeks to teach you how to use the fishing spear. This seems like a good time."

"Awesome!" I cried. I turned and kicked my way towards the ladder at the stern of the boat.

The *Cassandra* is a long white boat, the size of a small house. It's actually a sea lab, three decks tall.

The lower deck has sleeping cabins for us and the crew, storage compartments, and the galley, where we cook our meals and eat together.

The main deck is filled with research cabins and study labs and all kinds of radar and computer equipment. At the front of the top deck is the pilot's cabin, with the wheel and other controls. Behind that is an observation deck with even more electronic equipment.

My uncle is a marine biologist. He studies tropical fish and undersea plants. He spends a lot of time looking for fish and plants that haven't been discovered yet.

Dr D helped pull me on to the deck. He laughed when I splashed water over the front of his white lab coat.

I tossed my snorkel, mask and fins into the metal bin near the rail. Then I pulled off the wetsuit and tossed it in, too.

My uncle's name is George Deep, but everybody calls him Dr D. Even my dad – his brother – calls him Dr D.

Dad says everyone called George that back when he was ten years old. That's because he was always studying bugs and soil and tree leaves and stuff, even when he was just a kid.

Dr D is short and thin. He wears thick

black-rimmed glasses, he has curly brown hair and a bald spot on top of his head, and the expression on his face is almost always serious.

He wears a long white lab coat with a dozen pockets. He looks just the way a scientist should look.

He put a hand on my shoulder and led me along the side of the deck. "How was the water?" he asked.

"Kinda wet," I said.

He chuckled. It was a little joke we shared.

He raised the long metal fishing spear. "Know what this is?" he said.

"A toothpick for a whale?" I replied.

He laughed again. "Let's get serious, Billy. This is a very dangerous weapon." He wrapped my hand around the end. "Hold it like this."

Yes! I thought. *The Undersea Mutant raises the Pulverizer – my Death Spear made of super-charged lightning!*

Dr D took the spear from me. He wrapped his hand around it and raised it over his head. "Billy, watch carefully. This is how you throw it. See how I have it balanced?"

He pulled back – and heaved the spear into the water. I watched it cut through the surface without making a splash.

Dr D had attached a long rope to the back of the spear. He used it to pull the spear on to the boat.

"It takes a while to get the feel of it," he told me.

"Get the right balance first. Then aiming it will be a lot easier."

He handed the spear to me. "It's heavier than you thought, isn't it?"

It's light as a feather to the Undersea Mutant.

"Yeah. Kinda heavy," I said.

He slid my hand closer to the middle of the shaft. "Hold it here," he said. "Go ahead. Get it balanced, then give it a try."

I gripped the spear tightly. I stared over the rail, into the sparkling water.

I took a deep breath. I pulled my arm back as far as it would go – and I *heaved* the spear with all my might.

"HELLLLLP!" a shrill voice shrieked from the water.

My little sister, Sheena!

"HELLLP! You HIT me!"

My heart skipped a beat. I let out a horrified cry – and gripped the railing with both hands.

No. Please. Tell me I didn't do it.

Gasping for breath, I stared down over the rail.

Sheena's black hair spread out like a limp jellyfish on the surface of the ocean. Was she floating face down?

No. She tilted her head up. "Hope I didn't *scare* you, Billy!" She raised the spear in one hand and waved it over her head, laughing.

"Sheena, that's not a good joke," Dr D said, shaking his head.

"Sure it was!" Sheena replied. "It worked!"

What a brat.

"You didn't scare me at all," I said. My voice cracked. I hoped she didn't notice.

Sheena is ten, and she likes to prove that she's the bold, brave one in the family. Maybe she *is* a little braver than me. But mainly she's just loud and annoying.

"Dr D," Sheena shouted, "you shouldn't let Billy play with sharp things. He'll poke his eye out."

I groaned. "Ha-ha. Toss up the spear and wait right there. I need the target practice."

"You couldn't hit the *ocean* from there!" she cried. Then she laughed at her own dumb joke.

"Come up here," Dr D called to her. "I need to talk to you both."

Sheena climbed on to the deck. She pulled off her mask and her wetsuit, straightened her red swimming costume, and shook out her hair.

We look a lot alike. We both have straight black hair. Mine is short, and hers comes down past her shoulders.

We're both tall and kinda skinny. We both have dark blue eyes and heavy dark eyebrows that make us look serious, even when we're not.

Sometimes people say, "You two must be twins." That makes me stick my finger down my throat and gag. Because first, I'm a whole two years older than she is and second, we're not alike at all.

Sheena doesn't like to pretend. She would stare at the Albino Electric Eel and say, "That's just a clump of seaweed."

No way she could share the amazing adventures of the Undersea Mutant. She only likes things that are *real*. How boring is that?

Sheena carried the spear across the deck and dropped it on my bare foot.

"OWWWW!" I screamed, hopping up and down.

"I *told* you to be careful with that thing," Sheena said.

"Maybe next summer, I'll invite my *other* niece and nephew to join me," Dr D said. "They get along."

"We get along fine," Sheena said. She wrapped her arm around my shoulders and gave me a big fake hug. "Don't we, Billy-Willy?"

Totally annoying, right?

"No more target practice for today," Dr D said. "Take your places. It's time to move. I just got the OK over the radio. And the navigation maps I've been waiting for arrived today via satellite. So we are ready for action!"

He turned and headed up to the pilot's cabin.

"Where are we going?" I called after him.

"Deep waters," he said. He looked back and frowned at us. "*Very* deep waters."

The engines roared. Dr D turned the wheel, and the *Cassandra* edged sharply into the waves.

Sheena and I took our places on a bench against the cabin wall. The boat rocked hard, and a strong spray washed over the railing.

Soon, we were crashing over the sparkling waves. A red-orange sun floated on the horizon. I turned back and saw the tiny island of Careebo vanish, a speck of yellow on the blue water.

About an hour later, Dr D locked the wheel. Then he led the way down to the galley for some lunch.

Normally, the *Cassandra* has a crew of three or four. But when Sheena and I visit in the summer, Dr D likes to give them time off.

He pulled out the grilled bluefish left over from last night's dinner and some sandwich rolls, and we sat around the small white table and ate fish sandwiches and drank papaya juice.

After lunch, Dr D pulled off his glasses and cleaned them with his napkin. "I'll tell you what we're doing," he said. "But you probably won't believe me."

He chuckled. "I'm not sure I believe it myself. But we're going to try to track down a sunken pirate ship."

My mouth dropped open. "You mean like *real* pirates?" I said.

Dr D nodded and slid his glasses back on. "People have been searching for this ship for over two hundred years," he said. "My workers back on the mainland think they have located it using acoustic imaging and laser mapping. They just emailed me all the info."

Dr D's eyes flashed. "Here's the amazing thing," he said. "If the sonar image is correct, we're actually not too far from where the ship went down."

Sheena and I nodded and waited for him to tell us more.

"The ship is called the *Scarlet Skull*," he said. "Perfect name for a pirate ship, right?"

He took a long sip of papaya juice. "According to legend, the ship sank in the late 1780s," he said. "And it took millions of dollars of jewels and gold treasure down with it."

"And we're going to find the treasure and be *billionaires*!" I cried. I jumped up and pumped my fists in the air.

14

Sheena grabbed me and pulled me back down. "Billy, were you *born* immature?"

"If we find the treasure, it will all go to the Careebo Dolphin Rescue Fund," Dr D said. "I'd be thrilled to find it. But I'm a scientist – not a treasure hunter."

"This is totally cool!" I said. I was so excited, I could barely sit still.

"How did the pirate ship go down?" Sheena asked.

Dr D scratched his head. "This is where the story gets weird," he said. "And this is what I want to investigate. The reports at the time said there were *two* pirate ships. They were sailing in view of each other. It was a calm, clear day. The ocean waves were flat and gentle. And suddenly, a swirling black cloud swept over the water. The *Scarlet Skull* sailed into the cloud – and disappeared."

"Huh? It just disappeared?" I said.

Dr D nodded. "I *told* you it was weird. The black cloud passed, and the pirate ship had vanished. The pirates on the other ship stood staring, waiting for it to reappear. But . . . it was never seen again."

Sheena and I stared at him. Neither of us spoke.

Dr D opened a file of papers he had brought to lunch and scanned them quickly. "The *Scarlet*

Skull belonged to a notorious captain named Long Ben One-Leg," he said. "Long Ben was very bad news."

I felt a shiver at the back of my neck. "How bad?" I asked.

"Well, some people believe that he was so evil, the sea just swallowed him up. Swallowed him and his entire ship to protect the world from his evil."

Dr D continued to skim the papers. "Here's a story that will give you a good idea of what Captain Ben was like. It seems he kept a big tub of hungry rats on the ship. When one of his men did something to make him angry, he tossed the guy into the tub. Then he sat back and watched the rats make lunch of him."

Sheena grabbed her throat and groaned. "Ohhh, that's way sick!"

"Sometimes when he was bored," Dr D continued, "he threw someone in the rat tub just for entertainment."

"They didn't have TV in those days, right?" I joked.

But when I pictured the hungry rats gnawing on some poor guy, I felt a little ill.

"So all the pirates drowned when the ship went down?" Sheena asked.

Dr D nodded. "The pirates drowned. The rats drowned. And the treasure sank with them."

He set the papers on the table and squeezed

Sheena's hand. "And there's one more part to the story. A very creepy part."

He stopped as if he didn't want to tell us.

We waited, our eyes locked on his. "Tell us," I said. "Please. Tell us!"

Dr D hesitated. I could see he was thinking hard.

"Well. . ." he said finally. "According to legend, the *Scarlet Skull* is haunted. Long Ben prowls the sunken ship – always awake, always alert – to protect the treasure."

I gasped.

But Sheena laughed. "Uncle George, you don't believe in *ghosts* – do you?"

Dr D gazed back at her through his thick glasses. He didn't reply.

"*Do* you?" Sheena insisted. "Do you really believe in ghosts?"

"He . . . he's not a *ghost*," Dr D muttered. "According to the legend, he's a *zombie*."

And suddenly in my mind, sounding so distant, so far away, I heard a soft, evil whisper: *"I'm waiting for you . . . I'm waiting."*

Did Sheena and Dr D see me shiver?

I don't think they noticed.

Of course, the whispered voice was only in my mind. My wild imagination taking off again. I was sitting there scaring MYSELF!

This is the perfect mission for the Undersea Mutant, I told myself. *Zombie pirates in a sunken treasure ship. Awesome!*

So why did my stomach suddenly feel as if I'd swallowed a huge rock?

"Tell us the truth," my sister said, pressing our uncle. "Zombies – true or false?"

That made Dr D smile. "I'm a scientist," he said. "I study the real world. I don't believe in zombie pirates."

The *Cassandra* bounced hard on the waves. We tilted forward, then back. I gripped the edge of the table to steady myself.

I glanced out the galley porthole. In the distance, I could see islands of dark, craggy rocks and tall purple cliffs.

"I don't believe in zombies," Dr D repeated. "But I have been *fascinated* by this mystery for years. And if we can find the ship, I can study the natural causes. I can determine what *really* made that ship go down."

Dr D jumped up. He collected our plastic dishes and dropped them into the tiny galley sink. "Come on," he said. "I want to show you something."

He led us up to the main deck and around to the starboard side. Normally, he keeps a small dinghy tethered to the side – a little boat for going onshore on islands.

"Whoa!" I let out a startled cry. In place of the dinghy, a tiny *submarine* floated beside the *Cassandra*.

"It's my own design," Dr D said. "Cute, huh? I call it the *Deep Diver*."

My heart was racing. Were we really going down to the bottom of the ocean in this little sub?

I leaned over the rail and studied it. It looked like a toy. Shaped like a real submarine. Bright yellow metal with a narrow hatch on top, big enough for only one person at a time.

I saw round glass portholes in front, back, and on both sides. Two big headlights in front. Twin thrusters at the back.

"The three of us should fit OK," Dr D said. "It'll be a snug ride. My little sub won't go long distances. But it'll take us down to the sunken ship – if we find it. And it has a little speed. I can get it up to five knots if I really push it."

Another dangerous mission for the Undersea Mutant! I thought.

I imagined myself in a furious sword fight with a zombie pirate. Then I saw myself swimming away in victory, pulling a huge treasure chest brimming with jewels behind me.

Actually, I felt a little shaky. I had a fluttering feeling in my stomach. I couldn't help it. I was scared. The *Deep Diver* looked so small and fragile.

I imagined it being swallowed by an enormous shark. Then I shut my eyes and I imagined a deafening crash. Shattered glass. I pictured a GREAT GREEN EEL crashing through a porthole!

It had me in its teeth! It wrapped its tongue around me. I was about to become *eel food*!

WHOA! BILLY – STOP!

Yes, I could dream up crazy adventures all day long.

But even with my great imagination, I couldn't dream up the *real* horrors that awaited us at the bottom of the ocean.

It all started the next afternoon.

A little after two o'clock, Dr D called Sheena and me into his computer lab on the main deck of the *Cassandra*. "I think we're very close," he said.

He was staring at four monitors. They had blue and green ocean maps on them. White dots moved across the screens.

He pointed to a white dot on the top screen. "That's us," he said. Then he moved his finger over a dark shape at the bottom of the screen. "That *could* be the sunken ship."

Sheena and I stared at the dark shape. It didn't look like a ship. It just looked like a black smudge on the screen.

Dr D tapped the smudge two or three times. Then he jumped up from his chair. "Let's go check it out!"

I swallowed hard. "You mean – get in the sub?"

Sheena pumped her fists in the air. "This is totally cool!" she cried.

I couldn't let her see how scared I was. I slapped her a high five. "Don't be scared, Sheena. Dr D and I can handle things."

"Funny," Sheena said, rolling her eyes. "That's about as funny as a shark bite."

I bit her arm. Not too hard. Just as a joke. She's so annoying.

When we came out on the deck, Dr D had already anchored the *Cassandra*. It was a bright day with puffy white clouds high in the sky. The blue-green waves lapped calmly at our boat.

Dr D led us to the little sub. He pulled open the hatch. We peered down into the small chamber.

"Lower yourself slowly," Dr D said. "There's plenty of room once you get in the cabin."

Sheena bumped me out of the way. "Ladies first," she said. She squeezed into the hatch and lowered herself quickly out of sight.

"Awesome!" her voice echoed up from the tiny chamber.

My turn.

The Undersea Mutant follows the call to adventure! I told myself. *Wherever danger goes, the Mutant follows!*

My foot missed the bottom ladder rung. I fell. Landed on my feet. "Ta da!" I made it look as if I meant to do it.

Sheena didn't see my clumsy move. She took the seat at the end and studied the control panel. She turned and grinned at me. "What do you think would happen if I pushed this button?"

"Sheena – *don't*!" I cried.

She laughed. "Just testing you. You failed."

What a pain. Always trying to prove that she's braver than me.

I dropped down next to her. The black plastic seats were jammed close together. The cabin ceiling was just a few centimetres over our heads.

I heard the hatch slam shut above us. Dr D lowered himself into the cabin and dropped into the seat next to me.

He leaned over the control panel. He threw a few switches. The cabin filled with orange light. He pushed a yellow button, and the engine hummed to life.

"This sub is so easy to pilot, a monkey could do it," he said.

"Does that mean Billy could do it, too?" Sheena cracked.

"Let me show you both," Dr D said. "This is the helm. It steers just like the wheel of a car. That yellow button is the ignition."

He tapped a round screen on the control panel. "That's the satellite navigation system," he said. "It's like the GPS navigation in a car – only it maps the ocean. And this screen next to it is the sonar echo display. It picks up any objects on the ocean floor."

24

He pointed down to his foot. "See the pedal? It looks like an accelerator, right? Push the top of it down with the ball of your foot and the sub goes forward. Push the bottom down with your heel and the rear thrusters come on, sending the sub back."

He grabbed the stick to the right of the wheel. "Pull up and the sub goes up. Pull down and we descend."

I swallowed hard. I felt a little seasick, and we weren't even underwater yet.

I won't be so stressed once we start moving, I told myself.

What would the Undersea Mutant do in this situation?

I was too excited and scared to think about the Undersea Mutant. "D-do you really think the pirate ship is down here?" I stammered.

Dr D studied the satellite navigation screen. "Let's find out, Billy," he murmured.

He lowered his foot on the accelerator and pulled the stick down. I heard the thrusters roar to life. I grabbed the sides of the seat as we splashed hard in the water.

We were sinking slowly. I stared out the porthole. The blue sky disappeared as water covered the glass.

Down. Down.

A string of bubbles rippled outside the glass. The water darkened as we dropped. Dr D

25

pushed a switch, and the orange lights inside our chamber brightened to yellow.

"My ears just popped," Dr D said. "How about yours?"

"I think my *eyes* just popped!" I said. I wanted it to sound like a joke. But I think I sounded a little scared.

"Do we have diving equipment?" Sheena asked. "If we find the ship, can we swim out and explore it?"

What a show-off! I thought. *She wants to swim at the bottom of the ocean?*

Dr D shook his head. "No room for diving equipment. If the pressure holds, we should be able to get very close to the sunken ship. We can see a lot from inside here."

If the pressure holds?

An hour passed. Then another hour. "We have to descend very slowly," Dr D explained. "Especially in this tiny tin can."

I wished he wouldn't call it a tin can. I gazed out at the twin beams of light. All I could see was the blue-green murk.

Finally, Dr D pulled the stick up and cut off the rear thrusters. We slowly stopped dropping. The sub rocked from side to side.

Dr D squinted at the monitor. "We're about a hundred metres from the ocean floor," he said. "Need to move forward now."

I saw strange black coral formations out the side porthole. Shadowy forms. *Like underwater ghosts,* I thought.

Dr D pressed the accelerator. The sub hesitated for a moment, then shot forward.

He mopped sweat off his forehead with the palm of his hand. "I'm pretty excited," he said, staring at the navigation screen. "I've studied all kinds of sea life. But I've never seen anything like this. I—"

The engine sputtered. It sounded like a power lawn mower shutting down.

"Whoa—" Dr D uttered. "What's going on?"

Silence now.

"No problem. It just stalled," Dr D said. He pushed the yellow ignition button.

The engine coughed, sputtered. Died again.

"Hey—!" I let out a cry as I saw a huge black cloud rolling through the water towards us.

Sheena saw it, too. "What's *that*?" she cried.

It moved quickly. No time to speed out of its way.

I watched it roll forward, like an immense black tidal wave. Blacker than ink. Blacker than anything I'd ever seen.

"Dr D—?" My voice came out in a choked whisper. I gripped the sides of the seat. I was panting so hard, I could barely breathe.

"Dr D—?"

The blackness swept into the sub. Icy cold. I couldn't see Dr D. I couldn't see Sheena. I couldn't see my own hands in front of me.

"Dr D?" I repeated in a tiny voice. "What is *happening*?"

"I . . . I don't know," he answered. "And I don't like it."

"I can't see a thing," Sheena said. "It's like I'm blind!" She grabbed my arm. "Did we float into some kind of cave?"

"No," Dr D replied. "We're not in a cave. I'm not sure what this is."

"M-maybe it will float past us," I choked out. I kept blinking, trying to see. I felt ill. I swallowed hard, trying not to gag.

Sheena squeezed my arm. She was actually scared.

"There are inky parts out in these deep waters," Dr D said. "But I've never seen anything like this. Let me get the thrusters going, and I'll try to steer us out of it."

I couldn't see him. But I heard him working the controls. He muttered to himself each time the engine sputtered and died.

"Whoa!" I let out a cry as we started to spin.

Sheena bumped hard against me.

The sub spun faster – round and round – and I felt it start to drop.

We whirled down, then back up, spinning faster.

I felt dizzy. I grabbed my stomach. I could feel my lunch rise up to my throat.

"I – I can't explain this," Dr D stammered. "Something is *pulling* us. Something—"

He stopped suddenly.

The spinning slowed. The darkness covered us.

I jumped and let out a frightened cry when I heard a loud noise close to me.

THWUPPPPP.

It sounded like when Dad opens a coffee can and the air pops out.

Then . . . silence.

I held my breath, struggling not to puke. Finally, the inky blackness started to lift.

"Dr D? Are we OK?" I asked in a shaky voice.

No answer.

Blinking, I struggled to see through the grey mist.

"Dr D? Uncle George? What's happening?" I asked.

"Can you get us back to the surface?" Sheena asked.

The lights flashed back on.

Sheena and I both let out shocked cries.

Dr D was gone!

8

A cold shiver stiffened my back. I stared at the empty seat next to me.

"NO! NO! It's *impossible*!" I screamed.

Sheena jerked her body around and looked up. "The hatch—" she murmured. "Is it open? Did he—?"

I jumped to my feet and pulled myself up to the hatch.

Locked tight.

"But – he couldn't vanish into thin air!" Sheena said in a whisper. "Dr D? Dr D?" She began shouting his name. "Can you hear us?"

Silence.

The sub rocked gently. The black cloud had completely lifted.

I slumped into Dr D's seat. Sheena and I stared at each other. I knew we were both thinking the same thing.

"That pirate captain and his ship," I said. "They disappeared in a black cloud – remember?"

31

"No, Billy – don't say that!" Sheena cried, grabbing my arm. "They were never seen again. Don't say that! Don't! We'll find Dr D. I *know* we will!"

"OK, OK," I said. "Let go of me. You're hurting me."

She didn't even realize she kept squeezing my arm. "Billy, what are we going to *do*?"

I didn't answer. I gripped the wheel hard and tried to fight my panic.

Here we were, suddenly *all alone* near the bottom of the ocean in this tiny submarine.

How will we find Dr D? How much air do we have? How do we get back to the *Cassandra*? Are all THREE of us going to disappear?

Every question sent shiver after shiver down my back. I gripped the wheel tighter, struggling to *think*.

Strong currents rocked us from side to side. The twin lights on the front couldn't cut through the dark waters.

"The radio!" I cried. "We can call for help." I reached for the radio receiver.

"Do you know how to work it?" Sheena asked in a tiny voice.

"No," I said. "But maybe I can figure it out."

I pushed the two buttons beneath the speaker. "Hello? Hello? Can anyone hear me?"

Silence.

"Hello?" I pushed more buttons. "Hello? Is anyone there?"

Silence. I couldn't even get any static.

"We're too far down," I said. "The radio won't work at this depth."

Sheena was hugging herself, trying to stay calm. "Well, get us back to the surface," she snapped. "If we can get back to the *Cassandra*, we can radio for help."

I leaned over the control panel. My hand trembled as I pushed the yellow ignition button.

"Hey!" To my surprise, the engine roared to life.

"Yes!" Sheena cried. "We've got power! Bring us up, Billy! Hurry."

I pushed my foot down on the accelerator. I pushed the stick up all the way.

"Whoa! What's wrong?" I gasped.

We nosed down hard.

My head hit the glass. I saw flashing bursts of red. I let out a cry of pain.

Sheena screamed.

I pulled the stick down, then up again. But we kept falling. Faster. As if a strong force was sucking us down.

"Pull us up! Pull us up!" Sheena cried, frantically slamming her hands on the control board.

I stared into the beams of light in front of us.

They were tilting down. "What is *that*?" I gasped.

"I . . . I think it's a ship!" Sheena cried. "A sunken ship! DO something, Billy! DO something! We're going to CRASH right into it!"

It was all happening too fast to think. The dark form of the sunken ship rose up in front of us.

"Stop! Stop! Stop!" I didn't even realize I was screaming the word over and over.

A hard bounce sent me spilling forward. I hit the control panel.

To my shock, the engine sputtered and died.

Through the murky water, I stared down at the sunken ship, tilted nearly on its side on the ocean floor.

I saw broken masts. Tattered sails covered in algae. A ragged hole the size of a car in the side of the bow.

"It's the pirate ship," I said. "The *Scarlet Skull.* Sheena – do you *believe* it? We found it!"

Staring straight ahead, Sheena tugged at her hair. "We're still dropping," she said. "You have to get us out of here. Can you do it?" She grabbed my arm.

"M-maybe," I whispered.

I stared down at the ship's deck, covered in barnacles. Brown and black coral and slimy green algae encrusted the walls. The ship's wheel lay on its side, cracked and rotted.

I pushed the ignition button. The engine sputtered but didn't start. The dark water bubbled all around us – and the sub dropped sharply.

"Oh, no! Oh, no!" I screamed. My head smacked the glass again as our sub hit the mossy deck of the old ship and bounced up.

My hands flew off the controls. A strong current pushed us forward. We rammed into the main cabin wall.

CRAAAAAACK!

We both screamed in horror.

Our sub just split open!

We're going to DROWN down here!

But no.

The sub was OK. Part of the *ship's wall* splintered. It cracked and fell away.

The sub floated into the ship. Into a vast cabin, seaweed clinging to the ceiling and walls. Hundreds of silvery fish – thin as needles – fed off the weeds.

Silence inside the ship. Our sub tilted and spun slowly, casting a murky light all around.

"I . . . I think we're trapped in here," I whispered. "I don't think we can get out."

I was totally losing it. I never admitted it, but I always counted on Sheena to be the brave one. But now, it was *impossible* to be brave. We were both terrified out of our skulls!

As I peered out into the ship's cabin, Sheena shoved me aside and grabbed the controls. "Get back, Billy. Let *me* try."

She pushed the ignition button once. Twice. The engine only coughed. She stamped down hard on the accelerator. And then froze.

I saw her blue eyes bulge. I turned to follow her stare.

We both screamed when we saw it.

The face. The grinning face in the water. Staring in at us.

I gaped in horror at the grinning skull. The top of its head was crusted with black crab shells and snails. Fat brown sea worms bulged inside its mouth and its empty eye sockets.

It pressed against the glass in front of us. A skeleton in a rotting shirt and torn trousers. Its horrible face stared in at us. Then it raised its bony arms ... clenched its bony fingers into two fists.

BAM. BAM.

I jumped as it punched the glass with both fists.

"It ... it's ALIVE. It's trying to break in," Sheena said in a trembling whisper.

BAM. BAM.

I jumped with each punch.

From somewhere deep in the sunken ship, I heard a low moan. Like an animal in pain. And then ugly moans all around us.

And as we stared in open-mouthed panic, a wall of skeletons floated up, pressing their skulls against the glass.

Skeletons in tattered clothes, algae growing on their skulls, black crab shells hardened over their bones.

Frozen in terror, I stared at the dark, empty eye sockets, their toothless grins, their cracked skulls, the worms and snails and crabs clinging to them.

BAM. BAM.

They lowered their skulls and smacked the glass with their foreheads. Again. Again.

BAM. BAM.

They hammered the glass with their skulls and their bony hands. I saw fingers break off and float away. But the grinning skeletons kept pounding . . . pounding.

I whipped my head around and saw more of them behind us, clinging to the sub.

Sheena grabbed my arm and squeezed it tightly. "Billy . . . we're surrounded. The pirates . . . they're *alive*! They're BREAKING IN!"

BAM. BAM. BAM.

"Don't you see? We woke them up!" I cried. "We woke up the pirates!"

"Billy, they're going to break the glass!" Sheena wailed.

Panic swept over me. My heart pounded as

loudly as the skulls on the glass. I couldn't think straight.

BAM. BAM.

I slapped wildly at the ignition button.

"It won't go, Sheena!" I cried. "It won't go!"

11

BAM. BAM. BAM.

The ugly skulls battered the glass.

Sheena's eyes were wild. Her face turned bright red. She pounded the control panel with both fists –

– and the engine rumbled to life!

"YESSSSS!" I cried. I shoved the stick all the way up.

BAM. BAM. BAM.

All around us, the skulls beat in a steady rhythm against the portholes.

I could feel the sub start to rise. The skulls jerked back. Bony hands scratched against the glass, then fell away.

"YESSSS!"

The skeletal pirates disappeared beneath us. Their animal moans followed us, then slowly faded from our ears.

The dark green water bubbled as the sub shot up. I held the stick in my trembling hand, pulled it as far up as it would go.

"We got away," Sheena said. "We're heading to the surface. I knew we would. I *knew* we'd be OK."

Despite my fear, I burst out laughing. It sure didn't take long for Sheena to get her old personality back!

But now the frightening questions whirred through my brain once again. . .

Can we find our way back to the Cassandra? *If we do, will we be able to radio for help?*

Where is Dr D? Did he really vanish *from this tiny sub? How can we find him?*

Did we really see dead pirates come to life? Will they come after us? How much oxygen do we have left?

Sheena and I stared through the porthole as if hypnotized. We watched the swirling water and didn't say a word.

Finally, two hours later, the *Deep Diver* bobbed to the surface. I blinked in the bright sunlight. The waves shimmered as we rocked gently on top of the water.

"We made it!" I cried, letting out a long breath.

Sheena peered out the porthole. "But where is the *Cassandra*?" she asked.

I felt all my muscles tighten. "We can find it," I said. "We didn't go far."

I grabbed the wheel and began to turn the sub slowly. I made the sub spin in a wide circle.

No sign of the sea lab.

"It has to be here," Sheena murmured. "It's . . . our only chance."

Ignoring my fear, I moved the sub in larger and larger circles. But no. Nothing but ocean. Endless ocean, as far as we could see.

We rocked on the water. The only sound now was the wash of the waves against the sub. We both stared out at the rolling waves. We didn't say a word.

Finally, I turned to my sister. "We're all alone," I said softly. "Dr D is gone. And no one knows we're out here."

Sheena frowned at me. "And what's the *good* news?"

There was none.

12

Sheena jumped up from her seat and stumbled to the back of the sub. "I'm opening the hatch," she said. She was already halfway up the ladder. "We can see better up there."

"Are . . . are you sure it's a good idea?" I called.

Too late. I heard the hatch lid pop. The sea sounds grew louder.

Sheena hoisted herself to the top. The sub rocked and bobbed. The wind roared.

"Can you see the *Cassandra*?" I shouted.

She didn't answer. I don't think she could hear me.

Finally, she lowered herself one rung and bent her head towards me. To my surprise, she had a smile on her face.

"An island!" she cried. "Billy, there's an island out there."

"How close?" I shouted. "Can we swim to it?"

"We *have* to!" she cried. "The ocean is calm. We can make it if we take our time."

We should have worn our swimming costumes, I thought. We were in jeans and T-shirts. But, of course, we didn't know we'd have to leave the sub.

A large fish slid past the porthole.

I imagined a school of killer sharks circling us, snapping their jaws hungrily. I pictured the zombie pirates rising up from the ocean bottom and grabbing us.

No, Billy. Don't think about sharks – or zombies.

I heard a splash. I turned and gazed up at the empty hatch. Sheena was already in the water.

"Courage," I whispered. That's the official slogan of the Undersea Mutant.

I searched the control panel. I found a lever marked ANCHOR. I pulled the lever down and heard a loud buzz. Some kind of electric anchor. At least the sub would be here, ready for our return.

I pulled myself up to the top of the hatch. Shielding my eyes with one hand, I squinted into the distance. Yes. A long yellow sand island. I could see some trees near the shore.

"Come on, Billy – *jump!*" Sheena called. She floated on her back alongside the sub.

"Coming!" I shouted. I tried to steady myself over the edge of the hatch. But my legs trembled so hard, I could barely stand.

"Jump!" Sheena yelled. "What are you waiting for?"

"OK, OK," I muttered. I took a deep breath, raised both arms above my head –

– and leaped.

"OWWWWWWW!"

I screamed as I hit the hatch lid. My leg scraped along the metal edge. Sharp pain shot up my left side.

I did a hard belly flop into the water.

The cold rushed over me. My leg throbbed with pain.

Splashing wildly, I raised my head. I grabbed the aching leg.

"Sheena—" I called. A wave washed over me. I shook it off and pulled myself up.

"Sheena – help me! I can't swim! I think I BROKE my leg!"

13

Sheena quickly swam over to me. "*What* happened?"

"I . . . banged my leg on the hatch," I moaned, ducking under a high wave. "It's the same leg that shark bit last summer. It really hurts. I think maybe—"

"Let me see," Sheena said. She grabbed the leg and twisted it.

"HEY! STOP!" I screamed.

"It bends at the knee," she said. "It's not broken."

"Since when are you an expert on legs?" I cried.

But she didn't hear me. She was already swimming towards the island with slow, steady strokes.

I had no choice. I had to swim after her.

I ignored the pain, lowered my head to the water, and began doing my famous breaststroke.

"Courage," I whispered again. Just a reminder to myself.

The water was cold, and the waves were pulling against us. I'm a good swimmer. But halfway to the island, my arms started to ache.

My cut leg throbbed. I sucked in breath after breath and forced myself through the strong current.

I don't know how long it took to reach the island. Maybe half an hour. It seemed a lot longer.

I fell on to the sandy shore, shivering, gasping for air. My chest felt ready to explode.

I lay on my stomach, my head resting on the soft sand, breathing . . . just breathing. When I finally looked up, I saw Sheena leaning against the curved trunk of a palm tree, in a thick clump of ferns.

With a groan, I pulled myself to my feet. My waterlogged jeans and T-shirt hung heavily against my body. I took a step – and let out a cry. "Ow. My leg—"

I raised the knee and tested the leg a few times. It moved OK, but it hurt each time I bent it. I limped a few metres towards my sister, groaning with each step.

"Here," Sheena said. "This just washed ashore. Maybe you can lean on it. You know. Use it as a cane."

She held up a long stick. I hobbled over to her and grabbed it. It was a long piece of bleached driftwood. The perfect size.

"Don't call it a cane," I told her. "It's the Mutant's Golden Staff of Invincibility. It was handed down to me by The Eternals."

She rolled her eyes. "Whatever."

I tried the driftwood cane out. Leaning on it, I could get around pretty good.

I glanced around the island. A narrow strip of yellow sand formed the beach. Beyond the beach, I saw clumps of tall grass and ferns. A thick cluster of palm trees hid the rest of the land from view.

Strange, I thought. *No seagulls on the shore. No birds chirping in the trees. What a weird, dead silence.*

"Come on. Let's explore." Sheena's voice cut into my creepy thoughts. "Billy, can you walk?"

"No problem," I said. Leaning on the cane, I followed her along the shoreline.

Our sandals crunched on the soft sand. We passed a wide patch of tall grass blowing one way, then the other.

"Oh, wow." Sheena stopped and raised her arm to block me. "I don't believe it!" she cried. She stared wide-eyed at the sand.

I followed her gaze. And gasped. "Footprints!"

They led from the water, across the sand, into the trees.

"Dr D!" I cried. "He . . . he made it to shore!"

Without another word, we began following the footprints. Sheena trotted over the sand. I limped after her as fast as I could, leaning on the drift-wood stick.

The footprints led along a narrow path that twisted through a thick grove of palm trees. Tall reeds and ropy vines lined both sides of the path. We had to step over fat grey roots that poked up like giant snakes from the sand.

I stopped to rest my leg for a moment. "Dr D!" I shouted, cupping my hands around my mouth. "Uncle George? Can you hear me? Are you here?"

No answer.

My eyes on the footprints, I trotted after Sheena. "Hey!" I let out a sharp cry – and stopped beside her.

We both stared through an opening between lush fern leaves. Stared at a man in a long black cloak with a hood pulled over his head.

Was it Dr D? It had to be.

"Dr D! It's us!" Sheena cried.

Why didn't he turn around?

I pushed the fern leaves out of the way with the stick. Then we both burst through, running over the sand to our uncle.

"Oh!" I gasped, and stopped short.

Sheena grabbed my arm.

And we both opened our mouths in screams of horror.

14

The stick fell from my hand. I grabbed it back and raised it in front of me. Could I use it to defend myself?

I didn't need it. The hooded figure in front of us wasn't going to attack. It leaned against a tree. Unmoving. A skeleton!

I let out a groan. "Ohhhhh, *sick!*" The long cloak was covered in crawling worms and insects. Bugs climbed in and out of the skeleton's toothless mouth.

Under the cloak, I saw a rotting shirt. On the shirt's pocket, I saw a red skull and crossbones.

"A pirate!" I whispered.

"But . . . it's impossible," Sheena said in a whisper. "These footprints . . . Billy, look at them. They're *fresh!*"

I glanced down at the sand. Yes. Fresh footprints. Still deep in the sand.

"No. No way. . ." I murmured. I watched the fat brown worms slither around the grinning skull.

A chill made my whole body shake. I couldn't take my eyes off that ugly face.

"Billy, didn't you hear me? Let's go!" Sheena shouted.

I shook my head hard, trying to clear my mind. Trying to shake away my panic.

Sheena grabbed my hand and pulled me along a twisting path. We hurried through the trees and vines back to the beach. I struggled to keep up with her, leaning on the stick.

The sun was now a red ball, low over the water. The late afternoon light turned the ocean red and purple.

A pretty sight. But there was no way we could enjoy it.

"Stranded on a tiny island with a disgusting dead pirate," I muttered. "Dr D is gone. And we have no way to get home. Could it get any worse than this?"

"Yes, it could," Sheena replied in a whisper. "I think it just did." And she pointed to the sand in front of us.

15

I held my breath and followed her gaze. "Oh, no!" I saw at least a dozen sets of fresh footprints in the sand.

"They all lead from the water," Sheena said softly. "They cross the beach and go into the trees."

"They are skeleton footprints," I said. "See? Bone prints."

We stared at them, then at each other.

"The dead pirates!" Sheena cried. "It must be them. The pirates who smashed their heads and fists on the sub."

She shuddered. "We woke them up, Billy. Don't you see? When we crashed into their ship, we woke them up. And now they . . . they *followed* us here!"

My mind spun. "We . . . we have to find a hiding place," I said. "Somewhere safe where we can try to think."

"Away from this beach," Sheena said. "Away from these footprints."

I stared at the bony footprints pressed into the sand. Once again, my imagination took off.

I pictured the dead pirates staggering out of the waves. I could see them shaking water off their rotted clothes. Walking stiffly on the sand, their bones creaking and cracking and grinding.

Searching blindly for Sheena and me.

We trotted over the sand. My leg felt better. But I used the long driftwood stick to help pull myself along.

"Sheena, look!" I pointed to a tall pile of grey rocks at the far end of the beach. "There might be caves," I said. "Or a good hiding place behind the rocks."

"Let's check it out," Sheena said.

We took two or three steps.

"Whoooooaaaa!" I let out a startled cry as the sand gave way beneath me.

My arms shot up in the air as I started to slide.

I was sliding down . . . falling . . . sliding . . . falling . . . sliding. . .

Sand flew all around me.

A deep hole. Some kind of sand pit.

My hands grabbed at the sides. But the sand flew through my fingers. Sand clung to my wet

clothes. Covered my hair ... my face ... my
EYES!

Sliding ... falling ... sliding...

"We ... we're being BURIED ALIVE!" I
screamed.

16

I landed hard on my feet. "OWWWWW!" Pain shot up my body. My legs gave way, and I fell hard on to my bum.

Brushing sand off my face, out of my eyes, I started to choke.

I saw Sheena drop on to the sand beside me. She began coughing and sputtering, shaking herself violently, throwing off sand.

I spat out a gob of wet sand. The sour, gritty feeling on my tongue made my stomach heave. I took a deep breath and held it.

"We . . . we're alive," Sheena muttered, furiously brushing sand from her hair.

I picked lumps of sand from my nostrils. I spat again. Then I gazed up.

The pit was deep. I could see just a sliver of sky at the top.

I used the stick to pull myself to my feet. Bending over, I brushed the wet sand off my T-shirt and jeans. "It's sticky," I said. "And smelly."

"Maybe it's a trap," Sheena said. "The pirates set this sand trap. They meant to capture us."

"No way," I said. "The pirates just got here – remember? They didn't have time to dig this deep hole."

"Well . . . *somebody* made it," Sheena said. She stared up to the top. "Maybe we can climb out."

She dug both hands into the sand wall and tried to pull herself up. The soft sand gave way, and she slid back down.

I tried next, digging my hands deep into the sticky wet sand. "Hey!" The sand crumbled, and I toppled on to my back.

"It's too soft," Sheena said. "Can't get a good grip."

"Maybe the stick. . .?" I said.

I shoved the stick into the pit wall high above my head. Then, holding on to it tightly, I tried to hoist myself up.

No. The sand collapsed on me. I came tumbling back down on to my knees. The stick fell and nearly hit me on the head.

We didn't give up. We kept trying. I gave Sheena a boost. She climbed on to my shoulders. Her legs wrapped around my neck, nearly choking me. She kicked sand into my face.

"Get off!" I cried. "You're too heavy! This won't work."

"We have to try," she said. "We don't want to be trapped down here for ever!"

With a groan, I started to push her up the sand wall.

But I stopped when I heard sounds above us. Voices. From the beach.

"Oh!" With a startled cry, Sheena jumped off me. She pressed her back against the sand.

I froze. And listened to the voices. Men's voices. And as they came closer, I could hear the words they were chanting . . . chanting deep and low. The same words, over and over in a frightening, slow rhythm. . .

"The bones, they crack; the bones, they creep.
The men come alive in the briny deep.
You ended our death, you ended our sleep.
The men come alive in the briny deep.
So come with us, come with the men,
Come meet your fate with Captain Ben."

17

Sheena covered her ears. I peered up at the top of the pit.

The chanting grew louder. The voices surrounded us. Closer . . . closer . . . until they were right above our heads. . .

"You ended our death, you ended our sleep.
The men come alive in the briny deep.
So come with us, come with the men,
Come meet your fate with Captain Ben."

Sheena and I pressed ourselves tightly against the pit wall. We tried to burrow into the sand.

But there was no place to hide.

I looked up – and saw the grinning heads staring down at us from all around the top of the pit.

My legs were trembling. I could feel my heart racing.

I counted more than a dozen of them. Most were grinning skeletons wearing plain woollen shirts and trousers or dark jackets and ruffled shirts. Their clothes were stained, and the shredded, rotting cloth barely covered their bones.

Even *more* horrifying, three of them had *faces*. Bloated, distorted faces swollen from the water, with cheeks sagging to their shoulders and eye sockets stretched too big to hold their eyes.

Their blubbery white lips moved like fat maggots. Scraggly clumps of long hair fell over the sides of their heads. Snails and clamshells clung to their scalps.

The pirates poked their heads over the pit and continued to chant. Their voices echoed off their bony ribcages.

"You ended our death, you ended our sleep.
The men come alive in the briny deep."

"What do you *want*?" Sheena screamed up at them. "Leave us alone!"

But they reached down for us. Reached with long bony hands. The fingers curled and uncurled like snakes. Some of the hands had knobs of skin attached. Patches of decayed green skin on the palms and fingers.

They smelled so putrid, like milk that's been sour for months! The smell floated down over us. I started to choke. I could taste it on my tongue!

They lowered a rope ladder into the pit. Sheena

and I had no choice. We didn't want to spend the rest of our lives down here.

I grabbed the rope and struggled to climb. When I neared the top, hard, bony hands wrapped around my shoulders. Then grabbed me under the arms. And with surprising strength, hoisted me out of the pit.

The pirate set me down hard on the sand. He wore a three-cornered hat covered in slime. Long purple worms crawled over the brim. He was a skeleton except . . . except . . . he had half a face.

Skin hung from the right side of his face and flapped against the cheekbone. He had a dark moustache – just half a moustache – which he kept twirling as he stared at me with one empty eye socket and one blue eye.

"Let *go* of me!" Sheena screamed. It took two pirates to drag her off the ladder and set her on the ground. "Let us go! Leave us alone!" she cried.

Moving stiffly, their bones cracking, they formed a circle around us. A tall pirate with sagging, bluish skin scratched his scraggly hair – and it *came off* in his hand.

"Ohh, sick," I moaned.

Their bones clattered. The pirates moved in closer, tightening the circle. No way we could make a run for it.

"What do you *want*?" Sheena shouted. "Let us go. We didn't do anything to you!"

"Unh unh unh." The pirate with half a face started to grunt. His ugly head bobbed up and down on his rotted shoulders. "Unh unh."

Arms hanging limply at their sides, the circle of dead pirates began moving around us. Slowly at first, then faster. Stepping stiffly, their eyes locked on us.

I groaned in horror as one of the pirates lost a bony foot. It fell off his leg, but he didn't stop. He limped on, keeping the circle moving. Spinning around us. A circle of ghastly dead men.

And then suddenly, the circle opened. The pirate with half a face stepped aside. The other pirates backed away.

And I stared in shock as two men approached.

A grinning pirate led the way. He wore a long black coat with gold buttons down the front and the gold stripes of a captain on the shoulders. He had a whole face, with a thin black moustache and a short black beard. He looked alive – except for the dead green eyes sunk deep in his head.

He carried a crutch in one hand and limped towards us. As he approached, the pirates stood back in fear.

Was this Captain Ben?

And beside him . . . beside him . . . with the pirate's big hand grasping his shoulder . . . *our uncle!*

"Billy! Sheena!" Dr D cried. "They got *you*, too!"

18

"Dr D!" I shouted.

I started to run to him. But two pirates leaped forward and held me back. Their bony fingers dug into my shoulders.

They smelled like week-old vomit. Again, I had to hold my breath to keep from gagging.

"Let me go!" Sheena cried. She thrashed her arms and kicked. But two pirates held her tight.

I stared angrily at the pirate captain. The dead eyes gazed back at me. They looked like soft eggs set deep in the sockets. He had a missing leg. He leaned heavily on his crutch. He dug the crutch into the sand and took a step forward.

"Let go!" Sheena slammed her elbow into a pirate's open ribcage. The bones cracked loudly, but he didn't let go. Instead, he tightened a bony hand around her throat.

"Don't struggle," Dr D said. "They're too strong."

"Ohhhh, he smells so pukey!" Sheena cried. She covered her mouth with her hand.

Captain Ben tossed back his head and uttered a booming laugh. His voice sounded as if it came from down a deep tunnel.

The laugh made all the pirates jerk straight up at attention. I watched one of the pirates pull a fat worm from his open nose hole. He studied it, then shoved it back in.

"Uncle George!" I cried. "How did you get here?"

He shrugged. "I . . . I don't really know, Billy."

His white lab coat was covered in stains. His trousers were torn at one knee. The left lens in his glasses was cracked.

"How long have you been here?" I asked.

He shook his head. "It's not clear to me," he said. "It's all a blank. I'm sorry. . ."

"But . . . what do these pirates *want*?" I asked.

The pirate captain shoved Dr D aside and limped up to Sheena and me. "Captain Ben asks the questions," he said in that low voice that thundered inside his chest. "Captain Ben *asks* the questions, and he *answers* the questions."

At these words, some of the skeletal pirates trembled and shook. Bones clacked and rattled. An eyeball hit the sand. Its owner moved to pick it up – and accidentally *stepped* on it.

Captain Ben turned from Sheena to me. An ugly

grin spread over his face. "So he's your uncle, is he? Would ye like to see your uncle survive?" he asked. "Would ye like Captain Ben to let your uncle live?"

So I was right. I was staring at Captain Ben One-Leg – the legendary pirate. The evil pirate who had been dead for over two hundred years!

"Y-yes," I stammered. "Of *course* we want Dr D to live!"

"Aye, I'll bet," Captain Ben said. He grabbed Dr D by the shoulder and slammed him into the trunk of a palm tree.

Dr D groaned and fell to his knees, grabbing his shoulder.

Captain Ben laughed. "I like to watch a man bounce – don't you?"

"No!" Sheena screamed. "Stop it! Let us go!"

Captain Ben's grin faded. He scratched his black beard. "Careful, girl," he said. "Being dead for over two hundred years has put Captain Ben in a very bad mood."

"I don't care!" Sheena shouted. "Let us go!"

"I'll not let any of ye go," he said, holding his wet-eyed stare on Sheena. "And ye'll not have your uncle back – until you give me what is mine."

I swallowed, thinking hard, my mind spinning. *What did he mean?*

I whispered to Sheena, "What does he want? What does he think we have? His lost treasure?"

"Are you looking for your treasure? We don't have it!" Sheena shouted to the pirate captain. "We never saw it. We don't have your treasure!"

A scowl spread over Captain Ben's face. "Ye'll not have your uncle back," he repeated, "until ye give me what is mine."

"You have to believe us!" I called to the pirate captain. "We don't have it!" I raised my stick as if it were a sword.

All around us, the pirates tensed. They lifted their bony arms. I could tell they were preparing to fight.

Captain Ben stared at the stick. "Ye've made your choice," he said through gritted teeth. "The *wrong* choice."

He waved his arm in a signal to his men. "Take them!" he shouted. "Show them what we call *pirate mercy!*"

With a rattle of bones, the dead pirates closed in on us.

19

"Run, kids!" Dr D shouted. "Don't worry about me!"

I spun away from him. The pirate with half a face stretched out his arms and tried to grab me.

I ducked – and darted right through his legs.

Another pirate bumped up to me. His ruffled shirt, torn to shreds, revealed nothing but ribs underneath. He raised his hands, ready to fight.

I swung the driftwood stick at him. It caught him in the chest. I heard his brittle ribs crack. He let out a muffled gurgle and staggered back.

I took off running. My sandals pounded the sand. I turned away from the water and headed to the trees.

Sheena? Did she get away, too?

I didn't dare look back until I reached the thicket of palm trees. I ducked into the shade, grabbed a tree trunk, and held on. I rested against the smooth bark, trying to catch my breath.

"Billy – don't stop," a hoarse voice said.

Sheena. From behind another tree. "Look. They're coming after us." She pointed through the trees.

The pirates were staggering and limping and lurching towards us.

I pushed myself off the trunk and leaned on the driftwood stick. We both took off, dodging through the thick grove, pushing ferns and vines out of our path.

I could hear the grunts and groans of the pirates as they chased after us. Did they really think we had Captain Ben's treasure? Did they think we hid it somewhere on the island?

"Sheena – wait up!" I called.

I started to run, using the stick as a cane. Each step made my leg throb. "But the Undersea Mutant doesn't know the *meaning* of the word *pain*!" I declared.

Would the Undersea Mutant run away from a bunch of ugly, dead pirates?

Of *course* he would!

Beneath the twisting palm trees, the ground became soft and covered with a blanket of mossy leaves and needles. The air grew cooler as I ran into deep shadows.

Breathing hard, I caught up with my sister. Ducking our heads under low vines, we ran deeper and deeper into the trees.

"Whoa! Stop!"

"What is it?" she asked breathlessly.

I pointed to the ground. "That's not a vine. That's a snake."

I squinted at it. Stretched out across the path, the snake was huge – at least one or two metres long! It had camouflaged itself, the same green-brown as the leaves on the ground.

As we stared, it arched its body and raised its head. And without warning – *attacked*, snapping its fangs.

I shoved the stick in front of it. The snake's jaws clamped down on the driftwood.

I didn't think. My fright just made me act.

I swung the stick high with the snake clamped on to it. The snake flew off and whipped high into the air.

I didn't see it come down. But I heard it smack palm tree leaves behind us.

Sheena spun around, as if expecting the snake to come slithering back to us. "Wow," she murmured. "Billy, that was *awesome*."

"They call me the Snake Whisperer," I said.

She didn't laugh. "Shhh. Listen."

I heard the grumbling of the pirates. Still following. They hadn't given up.

"They're close by," Sheena whispered.

"Maybe we can find those tall rocks," I said. "They looked like a good hiding place."

"NOOOO!" Sheena let out a cry – as two men jumped out from the trees and blocked our path.

"You're not going anywhere," one of them said.

20

The men took a step towards us.

"Not going anywhere? Wh-why not?" I stammered.

"Because this is the end of the path," one of the men said. He smiled. A gold tooth gleamed in his mouth. "You can't go any further."

I stared at them. They were probably in their twenties. They both had short light brown hair and dark eyes.

Their faces were tanned. The one with the gold tooth was tall and lanky, about a foot taller than the other.

They wore khaki cargo trousers and striped polo shirts. They had brown leather camera cases strapped around their necks.

"You don't *look* like pirates," I said.

They squinted at us. "Pirates? We're photographers," the shorter one said.

He pulled a fat orange bug off my shoulder. I jumped back.

71

"Careful," I whispered to Sheena. "This could be a trap."

They overheard me. "What kind of trap?" the tall one asked.

"The pirates . . . they're chasing us," Sheena said, glancing back along the path.

The tall one smiled again, his gold tooth glowing. "Is this some kind of kids' game?"

"No," I said. "It's real."

"Real pirates? You're joking. Tell us the truth," he said.

"How do we know we can trust you?" Sheena demanded. "Who are you? What are you doing here at the end of the path?"

"Calm down," the tall one said. "I told you, we're photographers. We are shooting little-known Caribbean islands."

"My name is Roger Baldry," his partner said. "And this is Goldy Munroe. That's not his real name. But everyone calls him Goldy. You know. Because of the tooth."

Goldy grinned to show it off.

On the other side of the trees, I heard low voices. I grabbed Sheena. "We can't stay here. They're coming."

"I don't know who's chasing you, but you can follow me," Goldy said. He turned and started to push his way through the tall ferns.

Roger pulled a blue baseball cap from one of his

pockets. He placed it on his head and followed his friend.

Sheena and I held back. Could we trust these men?

Did we have a choice?

I followed them into the trees. The sun was setting. The ground grew swampy, and I kept staring into the sand, on the lookout for more snakes.

Sweat poured down my forehead. My clothes were drenched.

We stepped out on to the beach. I took a deep breath of the cool ocean air. I wiped my face with the sleeve of my T-shirt.

Roger and Goldy led us to a wall of grey rocks near the shore. Behind the rocks, I saw a small white motorboat bobbing in the water.

Sheena and I leaned against the rocks, catching our breath. I peered around the side. No sign of the pirates.

"What are you two kids doing here?" Roger asked, mopping his face with a red handkerchief. "Who brought you to this island?"

"Our uncle," I said. "I mean, he didn't bring us. He disappeared. We thought maybe—"

Goldy squinted at me. "Your uncle disappeared? Were you on a boat?"

"A mini sub," I said. "But it stalled out. The pirates woke up. They came after us. I mean, they followed us here."

Goldy put his hands on my shoulders. "Take a breath, kid. Get some oxygen to your brain. You're not making any sense."

"Yes, he is!" Sheena declared. "Our uncle disappeared from our sub. Billy and I had to swim here. But we woke up Captain Ben's dead pirates. They followed us here. And—"

Roger's eyebrows went up. His mouth dropped open. "Captain Ben? You mean Long Ben One-Leg?"

"Yes, of course," Sheena snapped. "His men captured us. Down the beach." She pointed.

"Captain Ben was there," I said, "with our uncle. He said we couldn't have Dr D back until we gave him what belongs to him. He wants his treasure."

Roger and Goldy studied us in silence. "You're not making this up?" Roger asked.

I shook my head. "No way."

"Then. . ." Goldy murmured, rubbing his chin. "Then . . . the legend is *true!*"

"Yes," Sheena said impatiently. "That's what we're trying to tell you."

"Do you have it?" Goldy asked. "Do you have his treasure?"

"No," I said. "We found Captain Ben's ship. We found the *Scarlet Skull*. But we didn't see any treasure."

The two men looked excited. Roger's face

reddened. Goldy studied us intently. "The pirate ship – where is it?" he asked.

"It's sunk offshore," I said. "Tilted almost on its side on the bottom of the ocean."

Goldy squinted at us. "Did you really find that old wreck? People have been looking for it for over two hundred years."

Roger gripped my shoulders. "Do you think you could find it again?" he asked.

They were both breathing hard. I could see their chests heaving up and down. Roger's face was bright red.

That made me suspicious. Maybe Sheena and I had told them too much.

"Are you after the treasure?" I asked.

Before they could answer, I heard a clatter above us on the rocks. I looked up – in time to see two skeleton pirates come leaping down.

Their long tattered coats flew up behind them as they sailed down on us. They raised rusted swords.

I grabbed Sheena and yanked her back. We fell on to our bums on the sand.

The two dead pirates landed on their feet in front of Roger and Goldy. They swung their jagged swords at the two men – *and sliced off their heads*!

21

No.

I blinked hard.

Terror can make you see crazy things.

Roger and Goldy still had their heads.

The two pirates swung their rusted swords again.

Again, Roger and Goldy ducked – and the blades whistled *inches* over their heads.

Then the two men dived at the pirates. Grabbed them around their waists, raised them high in the air – and *heaved* them into the rocks.

The pirates didn't utter a sound as their bodies fell apart. I watched the skulls fly off, the ribs separate, the leg bones roll away.

Roger and Goldy bumped knuckles. Roger picked up his baseball cap from the ground. Then they lifted Sheena and me to our feet.

"We'd better hurry," Goldy said, gazing down at the two piles of bones. "I bet more of these guys are on the way."

They turned and started to their boat.

"Wait," I said, trotting after them. "You didn't answer my question. Are you after Captain Ben's treasure?"

They both shook their heads.

"We don't want the treasure," Goldy said.

"These waters belong to the government. That means the treasure does, too," Roger said. "There's no way we want that trouble."

"Let the treasure stay at the bottom of the sea," Goldy said. "If Roger and I can take pictures of the sunken ship, we could sell them for a fortune."

"Goldy and I would be the most famous photographers in the world!" Roger said.

They continued to the motorboat, which was rocking gently on the waves. "We have our diving equipment onboard. Think you two can find the old sunken ship again?"

"Maybe," I said. "It's right under our mini sub."

Sheena frowned. "But that doesn't help us with our problems," she said. "How do we rescue our uncle George from the pirates?"

"Let's make a deal," Goldy said. "You guide us to the *Scarlet Skull*. We'll haul the treasure chest on to our boat. We'll bring it back for you to give to Captain Ben."

"Then we'll take the three of you wherever you want to go," Roger said. "Deal?"

They both stared at us, waiting for our answer.

"What are we waiting for?" I said. "Let's go."

Goldy and Roger splashed into the water, holding their camera cases high. Sheena and I followed. We waded to the boat. The warm water lapped over our waists.

Howls rang out from the beach. I turned and looked back. The pirates were coming after us, clambering into the water. They were shrieking like wild animals, swinging swords above their heads.

Goldy and Roger reached the boat. They grabbed the deck railing and hoisted themselves inside. Sheena climbed in easily. I tossed my walking stick on to the deck.

The motor started with a roar. I reached for the deck rail – and missed. I tumbled face-first into the water.

The pirates' howls grew louder. Closer. I floundered in fear, slapping at the water, struggling to stay on the surface.

The motor churned up the waves, sending a spray high in the air. The spray washed over the charging pirates.

Sputtering, I reached for the deck rail again. Caught it! I lifted myself – soaking wet – on to the deck.

Bony hands shot up from the water. Grabbed the deck rail. The pirates were climbing onboard!

The motor roared. The boat shot forward. We lifted off the water and zoomed away from the shore.

I struggled to keep my balance. I turned to the deck rail and shuddered. *Their bony hands were still gripping the rail.*

"Sheena – look!" I pointed to the hands, eight or nine pairs. "We didn't lose them. They're – they're coming with us!"

The boat lurched – and tilted to the side. I went stumbling to the rail. I couldn't stop myself. I grabbed for the rail – and my fingers wrapped around the cold, clammy hand of a skeleton pirate!

Unable to let go, I opened my mouth in a cry of horror.

22

Gripping the rail, I stared at the hands.

Just hands. No arms attached, or bodies.

The bony fingers clung to the rail, taking a sea ride with us. The arms and bodies, detached now, floated and bobbed in our wake.

Sheena pulled me away from the side. "Billy, sit down," she said. "You're drenched and you're shaking. You look totally wrecked."

I sat down and hugged myself. "I'm OK," I said weakly. "It's just . . . those hands." I shivered.

"Cheer up," Sheena said. "Roger and Goldy are going to help us. We'll get the treasure to Captain Ben. He'll set Dr D free. And they'll take us to the *Cassandra*."

I forced a smile to my face. "Sounds like a plan," I told Sheena. And then I gasped.

One of the skeleton hands was gripping my ankle!

Sheena pulled it off and tossed it into the water.

* * *

The boat rocked and tossed as it pushed through the waves. The evening sun sent stripes of deep red through the water. It would soon be dark.

Goldy carried a couple of long duffel bags from the cabin.

"The *Scarlet Skull* can't be far from here," Sheena said. "Billy and I swam to shore from the sub."

Goldy heaved the two bags to the stern. "One is our diving gear," he said. "The other is our cameras. We'll find the ship first, then come back for our photo equipment."

He walked to the rail. He plucked the skeleton hands off – one by one – and tossed them in the sea.

I climbed to my feet and watched Roger in the cabin. He stood behind the wheel, his cap pulled low over his eyes.

"There it is!" Sheena's shout made me jump.

Yes!

Our tiny sub bounced in the dark waves just ahead of us. The yellow hatch gleamed in the dying sunlight.

"Time to dive," Goldy called to Roger. "Anchor the boat."

Roger came bolting out of the cabin. "It's right down there?" he asked, pointing. "Captain One-Leg's old ship?"

"Yes, it should be close," I said.

The two men pumped their fists in the air. They

lowered the anchor over the stern. Then they pulled out scuba tanks and began tugging on wetsuits and fins.

Goldy turned to Sheena and me. He flashed us a thumbs up. "This is a great day," he said. "Roger and I are going to photograph that shipwreck and find the treasure so we can rescue your uncle."

We both returned the thumbs up.

They flashed on the halogen beams on their masks. Then the two men dived over the side. They disappeared quickly into the black, rolling waters.

Sheena and I leaned over the rail. We watched until the darkness swallowed them. Sheena shrugged. "Nothing to do now but wait," she said.

"*You* can wait. The Undersea Mutant must *always* be on the alert," I told her. I turned and made my way into the cabin. *I'll man the wheel till they get back*, I decided.

I stepped behind the wheel. A high wave made the boat rock. I fell back – and kicked one of their duffel bags.

It flipped on its side and fell open. "Huh?" I stared in shock.

Two small silver pistols tumbled out. No camera.

"Weird," I muttered. I grabbed the other duffel bag and fumbled it open.

Three pistols and a box of bullets.

I had a heavy feeling in my stomach. My throat suddenly felt dry.

I ran back on to the deck. I hurried to the stern and lifted one of the big duffel bags.

"What's up?" Sheena called, hurrying over to me.

"Goldy said there was camera equipment in here," I said. I tugged the bag open and dumped the contents on to the deck.

Rifles. Six or seven long-barrelled rifles clattered at my feet.

I let out a shuddering sigh. "Sheena," I whispered, "those two men. . . They lied to us. They're not photographers."

23

My legs suddenly felt weak. I grabbed the rail. I took a deep breath and held it.

Sheena pressed her hands to her cheeks. She stared at the rifles on the deck. "Billy . . . what are we going to do?"

I had an idea. "The radio!" I said. "Maybe we can radio for help."

I raced into the cabin. The radio stood on a shelf beside the wheel. I threw a switch.

A few seconds later, loud static poured from the speaker. I lifted the microphone to my mouth. "Can anyone hear me?" I shouted. "Hello? Can anyone hear this?"

I turned a few dials. "Hello? Can anyone hear me?"

Just static.

"Come on, work! Please work!" I cried. I turned dials and threw switches.

"Billy – they're *coming up*!" Sheena shouted from the deck.

My breath caught in my throat. Who were these two liars? What did they *really* want?

I ran across the deck. I stepped beside Sheena at the rail. Roger and Goldy bobbed to the surface. Water dripped down their masks.

I leaned over the side and squinted into the darkness.

Between them they held a big black chest with a sparkling red jewel on the lid. Even against the night sky, the jewel glowed brightly.

I could see it clearly. A glowing scarlet skull.

They raised the chest high and hoisted it on to the deck. Then they lifted themselves on to the boat. They shook water off their wetsuits.

"We found the treasure!" Goldy said.

"And we're keeping it," Roger added. "It's ours." He started to pull off his mask. But he froze when he saw the rifles strewn on the deck.

"Uh-oh," he muttered. "I see you two have been snooping in places you don't belong."

"You – you *lied* to us!" I cried.

Goldy shrugged. "It's a tough world, kid."

He pulled up his diving mask. Sheena and I both let out cries. His *face* came off with the mask!

We were staring at a grinning skull. A skull with a gold tooth hanging from its mouth.

Roger pulled off his mask and tossed it on to the deck. His face didn't come off. But the skin came loose around his mouth. He tried to push it back into place.

"Who – who are you?" I stammered.

"We were on the ship that watched the *Scarlet Skull* disappear in a black cloud," Goldy said.

"Disappear with *our* treasure. Captain Ben stole it from us," Roger said. "We dived into the water to get it back. But we never made it to the *Scarlet Skull*. That black cloud carried us away, and we've been lost – till now," Roger said.

"We're *rich*!" Goldy said. "After over two hundred years of searching for this, it's OURS again!" He tossed back his skull and uttered a dry laugh.

"These outfits came in handy," Roger said. "Goldy and I were so cold in our bare bones all these years. We stole the clothes from a couple of fishermen, and we took their boat, too."

A smile spread over his face. "Then we took their *skin*."

My stomach lurched. I had to force down my lunch.

Sheena's mouth hung open. She tugged at her long hair. "You're really going to *keep* the treasure?" she asked in a tiny voice.

"Yes. And thank you from the bottom of our hearts," Goldy said. He gave us a two-fingered salute.

"We owe you our gratitude," Roger said. "And now, sadly, we must say goodbye to you both."

"Goodbye?" I cried. "What do you mean?"

They didn't answer.

Goldy just shrugged.

Roger moved quickly. He lifted Sheena off the deck – and tossed her overboard.

24

I heard the splash as she hit the water.

The sound sent chills down my back. "You can't *do* that!" I screamed.

I raised the driftwood stick and swung it at Roger with all my strength.

Roger ducked. The stick grazed his back. It pulled off a big chunk of skin. With a grunt, he grasped me around the waist.

I put up a pretty good struggle. But he was too strong. He shoved me against the rail – *then flipped me into the sea.*

I hit the water hard on my stomach and went under. The cold sent a paralysing shock over my body.

Finally, I raised my arms and forced myself to the surface. Coughing and sputtering, I searched for my sister. I spotted her a few metres behind me. She was struggling to stay on top of the waves.

"Help us!" Sheena screamed to the two pirates. "You can't let us drown here! *Help* us!"

They turned their backs.

"Help us!" Sheena screamed. "Don't leave us!"

I frantically tried to keep afloat. I watched the two men. They were leaning over the treasure chest. I could see the scarlet skull glowing against the night sky.

Roger reached down to open the chest. He was about to grab the scarlet jewel.

The red skull glowed so brightly, I could see everything clear as day.

I saw Roger grab the skull. I heard Goldy scream, "NOOOOO!" I saw Goldy try to tug Roger away.

Too late. The red skull snapped open its jaws – and BIT Roger's hand.

And as the jaws clamped down, a fireball of white light burst over the boat. So bright, the sea lit up all around us.

And a powerful red current – like red lightning – blazed over both men.

BZZZZZZZZZZZZZZZT!

For a second, their bodies lit up. I could see the *bones* under their skin!

Trapped inside the crackling current, Roger and Goldy did a terrifying dance. Their arms flew wildly over their heads. Their whole bodies shook and shimmied.

And then. . . And then . . . their *heads* flew off their bodies, high into the fiery sky.

Both men crumpled to the deck, twin piles of bone and ash.

The buzzing, crackling red current faded to black. Sheena and I were alone in the sea now, thrashing our arms and legs, shivering in the cold.

"Come on," I choked out. I swam to the boat. Grabbed for the deck rail. And pulled myself onboard.

Shivering, I saw the driftwood stick on the cabin floor. I grasped it in both hands. I held it out to Sheena. She grabbed on, and I pulled her to the deck.

We both sprawled on our backs, our chests heaving. I shut my eyes and waited for my breathing to return to normal.

I sat up, blinking away water. Down the deck, the wind was blowing hard, carrying away the two pirates' ashes.

My legs were shaky and sore, but I managed to stand up. "Sheena, maybe our luck is changing," I said.

Before she could answer, a hard *BUMP* jolted the boat.

BANNNNNG!

Something hit us. *BANNNNNG!* Again.

I lost my balance. I staggered and fell. "Ow!" My head smacked the deck.

Another *BUMP*, even harder this time.

And everything went black.

25

"Billy – I don't *believe* it!" Sheena cried.

Her shout cleared my head. Shaking off the pain, dizzy, I climbed to my feet.

"Look!" She pointed out to the water.

I slowly turned and saw another boat bumping against us. I recognized it instantly. The *Cassandra*!

"It . . . it must have come loose from its anchor," I said. "It bumped right into us."

The *Cassandra* pulled alongside, as if it had come to *meet* us!

We both cheered.

"Sheena, help me carry the treasure chest on to the *Cassandra*," I said. "We'll return it to Captain Ben on the island. And he'll let Dr D go."

We each grabbed a handle and began carefully sliding the chest across the deck.

"Be careful. Don't touch the scarlet skull," Sheena warned. "You saw what happens when the skull bites!"

I shuddered. I pictured the two pirates doing their horrifying death dance inside the red streaks of electricity.

I hoisted myself on to the *Cassandra*. I pulled and Sheena pushed. We shoved the chest on to the deck of the boat.

Sheena hopped on to the *Cassandra*. We cheered and touched knuckles. It felt good to be home!

We had the treasure with us. Now we just had to use it to rescue our uncle.

I stepped into the cabin. I began to throw switches, powering up the controls. I pushed the ignition. The engine started up instantly.

I grabbed the wheel. Of *course* I knew how to pilot the *Cassandra*. The Undersea Mutant can handle *any* boat on *any* sea!

Besides, I didn't have to take it far. The island stood only a few minutes away.

I eased the throttle forward. The boat began to move, cutting through the waves. I could see the island on the navigation screen. Piece of cake.

Or was it?

Suddenly, the boat began to rock. The wind howled around the cabin walls. Tall waves tossed up in front of us and pushed us back.

Sheena burst into the cabin. "Billy – what's *happening*?" she cried.

I kept my hands on the wheel. The boat tilted up hard, then crashed back down into the heaving waves.

"Why is the sea going crazy?" Sheena cried.

I didn't have to answer. We both saw it at the same time.

An *enormous* ship, rising up from under the water. Its sails billowed and stretched against the wind. Its prow rose and fell as it bounced on the waves.

The ship came sailing straight at us!

Sheena's eyes bulged. "Billy – it can't be! Do you recognize it? The ship – it's the *Scarlet Skull*!"

"It's going to crash right into us!" I screamed. I whipped the wheel to the right as far as it would go.

Too late.

The *Scarlet Skull* rose up like a skyscraper in front of us.

And standing at the bow, I saw Captain Ben. His long black coat flapped behind him in the wind.

"Oh, wow! I don't believe it!" I cried.

The pirate captain had his arm wrapped around Dr D!

"Dr D? Are you OK?" I shouted.

"Don't ask questions!" Captain Ben boomed down at us. "Do ye want yer uncle returned? I'll give ye scurvy dogs one more chance to give me what is mine!"

"OK, OK," I cried. I shoved the treasure chest to the edge of the deck. "Here. Take your treasure! We don't want it!"

Above us, Captain Ben shook his head. *"Give me what is mine!"* he screamed.

"Take the treasure! Take it!" I shouted.

Captain Ben shook his head again. He raged his fists in the air. "I don't want the treasure! I WANT MY *LEG!*"

Leg?

He pointed furiously to the stick in my hand.

Huh?

I wasn't leaning on a long piece of driftwood. All this time, I'd been carrying around Captain Ben's LEG!

It was his *leg* he wanted returned!

I raised the leg bone high. I pulled my arm back to toss it up to him.

But Sheena held me back. "Captain Ben!" she shouted. "If we give you the leg, how do we know you'll return our uncle?"

Captain Ben tossed back his head and laughed. "Return your uncle? Don't ye know what a notorious *liar* I am? I'll take my leg – *and* my treasure! And then all three of ye will be joining me *at the bottom of the sea!*"

Not a chance, I thought.

He'll never take us down with him.

No zombie pirate can outsmart the Undersea Mutant!

Suddenly, I knew what I had to do.

The long leg bone trembled in my hand. I wrapped my fingers around it tightly. I remembered Dr D's spear-fishing lesson.

I shut my eyes and repeated in my mind what I had learned.

Balance . . . aim . . . power.

I took a deep breath. I pulled the bone back like a fishing spear. I aimed carefully. And I *heaved* it up to the deck of the pirate ship.

"YAAAAIIIIII!"

Captain Ben let out a ferocious howl as the bone smashed into his chest – *and pierced right through him*!

It was stuck inside him. The sharp end of the bone poked out his back.

Captain Ben howled in agony. He grabbed the front of the bone with both hands – and tried to pull it out of his chest.

"YAAAAAIIII!" Another scream echoed off the water. He tugged so hard at the bone, *he pulled himself overboard*!

Sheena and I hugged each other and watched him splash into the water. He slapped at the surface for a few seconds. Then he sank out of sight.

He didn't come up.

Suddenly, tall waves rocked our boat. The sea began to toss and swirl all around us.

"Billy – look!" Sheena cried. "The *Scarlet Skull* . . . it's CRACKING APART!"

Yes. The old ship began to crack and crumble. The sails fell apart, pieces flying away like a million feathers.

The masts split and fell. The ship walls crumbled to sawdust and dropped into the sea.

Within moments, not a trace of the ship remained.

"Dr D—!" I shouted. "Dr D! Where are you?"

Sheena gasped. "He . . . he went down with the ship! He's GONE!"

27

I gripped the rail and stared out at the tossing waters.

"Dr D! Dr D!" I shouted his name again and again.

No sign of him.

Sheena covered her face. Her shoulders trembled up and down.

And then I saw a hand reach up to the deck. It grabbed the side of the boat. Another hand appeared beside it.

I leaned down and helped Dr D into the boat. He climbed to his feet quickly, shivering and shaking off water.

"You're *safe*!" Sheena cried. We both rushed to hug him. "You're safe! You're safe!"

"No time," he muttered. "We're *not* safe."

He turned and watched the shredded sails sinking into the tossing waters. "Let's get the treasure chest down below. We've got to get out of here."

We pushed the chest to the lower cabin. Then

Sheena and I jammed in beside Dr D and he started the *Cassandra*.

Walls of water rose all around us. Our boat tilted up high, then slammed back to the surface.

"We have to find that black cloud," Dr D said, gripping the wheel with both hands. He pushed the throttle forward as far as it would go.

"The black cloud?" I cried. "You want to find it again?"

"When we went through it, we entered a Dead Zone," Dr D explained. "That's what the old legends say. And I'm starting to *believe* them! We have to go through it again and get to the other side. This isn't our world. We're in the world of the DEAD!"

My mouth dropped open. A shiver shook my whole body.

Dr D is a scientist. I knew he never believed any of this stuff. But we had all seen it with our own eyes!

"That's why the pirates came to life?" Sheena asked.

Dr D nodded. "And that's why in over two hundred years, no one has ever found the *Scarlet Skull*. It lies in the realm of the dead. And we will, too – unless we can travel back through that cloud."

The *Cassandra* roared forward. Above us, a pale full moon drifted low over the ocean. Were we travelling in the right direction? Was there a way back to our world?

We didn't speak. We stared straight ahead. The pale moonlight made the waves glimmer grey and dark green.

And then suddenly, the moon vanished. The light died. The water faded to black.

Total darkness. A thick, choking blackness.

I tried to speak. But the darkness swallowed all sound.

We found it, I thought. *We found the black cloud, and we're sailing through it!*

When a full white moon finally appeared in the sky, all three of us cheered.

We hugged one another, laughing and shouting. And did a wild, happy dance on the deck. It was the best celebration of my life!

"The treasure!" Dr D cried. "We're safe now. Let's check it out."

I led the way down the steps to the cabin – and gasped in shock.

"Gone!" I cried. "The chest – it's gone!"

Dr D scratched his head. "Oh, well," he said. "We came back safe – but empty-handed."

Just a typical day in the life of the Undersea Mutant! I thought.

And then I spotted something sparkle on the cabin floor. The skull! The red-jewelled skull!

"Check it out!" I shouted. "We *didn't* come

back empty-handed!" I reached down to pick it up.

"Billy – DON'T!" Sheena cried. "Don't touch it! Did you forget? It bites!"

"Don't be crazy," I said. "We're back in the land of the living. Now it's just a plain, ordinary jewel."

I picked it up – and opened my mouth in a deafening howl of agony. "YOOOWWWWWWWWW! It BIT me! It BIT me!"

Sheena leaped back in horror – and screamed at the top of her lungs.

I laughed and tossed the big jewel from hand to hand. "Just kidding," I said. "This time, I really gotcha, Sheena!"

I handed the scarlet skull to Dr D. "Guess this adventure is over," I said.

"Guess it is," he replied. "I'm going to radio the base and let them know we're OK."

We followed him up to the control cabin. He switched on the radio and turned a few dials. "Dr D to base," he said into the microphone. "Dr D to base. Can anyone hear me?"

We heard a crackling sound. And then from the speaker, we heard low voices:

"The bones, they crack; the bones, they creep.
The men come alive in the briny deep.
You ended our death, you ended our sleep.
The men come alive in the briny deep."

ENTER
HORRORLAND

The Invitation

DEAR BILLY & SHEENA DEEP:

You are in DEEP trouble now! Don't SCREAM—but you have won a free, week-long stay at HORRORLAND Theme Park, the SCARIEST Place on Earth!

Bring your PARENTS. Bring your swimming costumes and your diving gear. And be sure to bring some shark food (like your hands and feet!).

We've enclosed FREE PASSES to our HUNGRY CROCS PIGGYBACK RIDE—where having fun is a SNAP!

And you'll enjoy a visit to the BAT BARN CAFÉ. Join our thirsty vampires there for a WARM DRINK!

You don't need a ticket for the 20-MILE SWIM-FOR-YOUR-LIFE RIDE. We know you'll find it BREATHTAKING!

Your luxury room at the STAGGER INN offers 24-hour TOMB service. Oops. Of course, we mean ROOM service!

Come be our guest. We look forward to SCARING you!

Please RSVP to:
Di Kwickley, Guest Relations

1

My sister, Sheena, and I were thrilled. Sheena was so excited about going to HorrorLand, she was nice to me for a whole week!

A lot of our friends had been there, and they told us all about it. They said it was the most awesome park on earth.

Sheena and I spent the morning just walking around the park, taking it all in. Believe it or not, the first thing I wanted to do was go on The Bottomless Canoe Ride.

I know, I know. Sheena and I had just had a *horrifying* time on the water. I guess that's one reason we were so happy to be in a place where the scares weren't real.

But we never made it to the Bottomless Canoe.

After lunch, we trotted through the hotel lobby – and saw two very unhappy girls at the front desk. They were about our age. Both were tall and thin with coppery hair.

One wore a pale green T-shirt over white tennis shorts. The other wore a short red-and-yellow sundress.

"But that's *impossible*!" the girl in the sundress cried. She pounded her hand on the front desk.

The Horror behind the desk shrugged. "Go figure."

"That's what you told us the *last* time!" the girl cried. "It *has* to be a mistake!"

Sheena and I stopped to watch. What was their problem?

The girls stepped away from the desk. One of them was trembling. The other one tried to comfort her. "Of *course* it's a mistake," she said.

Sheena can never resist trouble. She pulled me over to the two girls. "What's wrong?" she asked.

They both jumped. I guess we startled them. "My parents are missing," the one in the sundress said.

"No big deal," Sheena said. "Our parents are missing, too."

They both gasped.

"Yeah," I added. "Who needs parents?"

I meant it as a joke. You know. Trying to get them to lighten up. But they didn't laugh.

They told us their names. Britney Crosby and Molly Molloy.

"Your parents are missing, too? For *real*?" Britney asked.

"Nothing is real here," I said.

We led them further away from the dude behind the front desk. "Don't be upset," Sheena said. "Our family checked in this morning. Outside my room, I heard some Horrors talking in the hall. They said they always sneak the parents away. To a hotel of their own."

"They did it to us," I said. "We went to our parents' room, and they were gone."

Molly shook her head. "You mean it's a joke?" she asked. "And then the Horrors lie and say your parents checked out and went home without you?"

Sheena nodded. "They do it to all the kids. It's one of their favourite scares. It's like everything else here. A big fake."

Britney let out a sigh. "I *knew* my parents wouldn't just leave," she said.

"You've never been here before?" I asked.

Britney and Molly shook their heads. "Britney got a special invitation," Molly said. "We were totally *psyched*."

"Us, too," I said.

I could see Britney was still worrying about something. "My dad left his new digital camera in their room," she said. She pulled it out of her bag.

"Can't you just return it when you see him?" I asked.

"You don't understand," Britney said. "He left a

picture in it. It was crazy. A . . . a picture of Slappy."

"Who?" Sheena and I both asked at once.

"A ventriloquist's dummy," Molly said.

"From back home," Britney added. *"No way* that picture could be in the camera. *No way* Slappy could be here in HorrorLand."

I stared at them. Britney was trembling. Molly looked really upset, too.

A ventriloquist's dummy? What's the big deal?

"Can we see it?" Sheena asked. "Show us."

Again, Britney glanced at Molly. They were definitely stressed. I figured there was something about this dummy they weren't telling us.

Britney raised the camera and clicked it on. She pressed a button and squinted at the view screen. "Weird," she muttered.

Molly grabbed Britney's arm. "What's wrong?"

Britney pressed the button again. Then again.

"The photo is *gone!*" she said. "No – wait!"

She let out a gasp. She held the camera up to her friend. "I don't believe it, Molly! Look!"

Sheena and I edged up behind Molly so we could see the photo, too. I squinted at the little screen.

And there we were in the photo . . . Britney, Molly, and Sheena and me. And the dummy was standing *right behind us*!

"How did you take this picture of us?" Sheena asked Britney. "The camera was in your bag." Sheena had her face all scrunched up, the way she does when she's puzzled.

Britney didn't answer. She stared at the screen. She was breathing really hard. She looked totally frightened. She glanced all around the lobby as if that dummy could be hiding in any corner. Imagine being afraid of an old ventriloquist's dummy!

Finally, Molly took the camera from her. "It must be some kind of HorrorLand trick," she said softly. "Forget about it. We came here to have fun."

"You got *that* right!" I said. "Here we are in the most awesome theme park on earth. Let's go out and go crazy!"

"I think I'm *already* going crazy," Britney muttered. She shuddered. Then she tucked the camera into her bag. "You're right. It's some kind of joke. Let's try to have some fun."

The two girls followed Sheena and me out into the park.

It was a sunny, breezy day. Zombie Plaza was crowded with families hurrying in all directions. I heard screams and laughter all around.

A Horror walked by carrying a bunch of helium balloons, all black. His purple tail bounced up and down as he struggled to hold on to the long strings in the strong gusts of wind.

"How about a balloon?" he asked, stepping in front of us. "What colour would you like? Black?"

Before we could answer, a blast of wind sent him stumbling away.

A female Horror came by wearing a black and white signboard. The big letters on the front read: FUN! THRILLS! THE FREE-FALL BUNGEE RIDE! The sign on her back read: ONE-WAY TICKETS ONLY!

She stopped and called to the four of us, "Want to try it? It doesn't hurt at all until you land!"

We laughed. I could see Britney and Molly were starting to cheer up.

"My friend Jason back home said we had to try The Bottomless Canoe Ride," Britney said. "He said you get *really* wet."

"Sheena and I were just talking about that ride!" I said.

Britney pointed across the plaza. "It's over there on the other side of Quicksand Beach."

"Yo! Quicksand Beach! *Yesss!*" I cried. I pumped

my fists in the air. "We've got to try that first. Think they have *real* quicksand?"

Sheena gave me a shove. "Haven't you had *enough* sand traps?"

"There's no such thing as enough," I said. I took off, running towards the big sign that read:

QUICKSAND BEACH. SINK . . . OR SINK!

As we ran closer, I could see kids up to their waists in the sand. They were screaming and frantically struggling to climb out.

I knew it *had* to be totally awesome.

We stepped up to the entrance booth. Sheena held back. "Billy, you're totally nuts. I can't *believe* you want to do this after what we went through with that sand pit."

"This time, it's just a joke," I replied.

A Horror leaned out of the booth. He asked our shoe sizes. Then he pulled out four pairs of blue rubber shoes and set them on the counter. "These are for walking on the quicksand," he said. "Of course, you won't walk very *far*!"

Molly tugged nervously at a strand of her hair. "What happens when we sink?" she asked him.

He handed her a pair of shoes. "If you go under, hold your breath as long as you can," he said. "Sometimes it helps."

We stepped out on to the wet yellow sand. Molly grabbed my arm. "He was joking – right?"

"Everything is a joke here – remember?" I said.

I took five or six steps. The rubber shoes made a *squish squish squish* sound. Clumps of sand stuck to the soles.

Quicksand Beach was a large square area of sand facing a tiny green pond. It was kind of like a big sandbox. The beach was fenced off on three sides. To keep innocent people from wandering on to it, I guessed.

"It's so soft and mushy, it's hard to balance," Molly said. She had her arms stuck out at her sides, like she was on a tightrope. "It's like walking on pudding," she said.

"It's kind of quiet here," Britney said.

I gazed around. The kids we saw earlier were gone. We were the only ones on the beach now.

Squish squish. . .

"WHOOOAAA!" I let out a shout as I felt myself start to sink.

The shoes were stuck in the mucky, wet sand. In seconds, my ankles disappeared. Then the sand rose up like a goopy ocean wave over my calves.

"Help!" Sheena twisted and squirmed, but she started to sink, too. It took only a few seconds for her knees to disappear. She was dropping fast!

I turned my head and saw Britney and Molly waving their arms frantically. They'd already sunk to their waists.

"Are we having fun yet?" Sheena asked.

I laughed. "It feels kinda weird, doesn't it? It's so lumpy and wet. I didn't expect it to be so *hot*!"

"I . . . I don't like this!" Molly cried. "It's like sinking in vomit!"

"Thanks for sharing that," I groaned.

I saw a human hand poking up from below the surface. I had to study it twice. It looked so *real*!

Sheena slapped my shoulder and pointed. "Check those out," she said. I followed her gaze and saw yellow bones – skeletons of small animals – trapped in the quicksand.

"Those skeletons. . ." Sheena said. "They look like . . . *rat skeletons*!"

"Totally fake," I said. But – *whoa*. I sank to my armpits in the mucky sand. I had to raise my arms high to keep them above the surface.

I tried to kick my legs, tried to raise my knees.

But I had sunk too deep. Every move I made forced me to sink lower.

"Hellllp—!" I heard Britney's shrill cry. "Isn't anyone going to rescue us?"

"Yeah. Who's gonna pull us out?" Molly's voice shook.

I felt myself drop. The sand rose up to my chin. A sharp, sour smell invaded my nostrils.

"Billy, help—" Sheena whispered. "This isn't fun. We're . . . gonna go under!"

"Isn't anyone w-watching us?" Molly sputtered.

I started to answer and got a mouthful of sticky, wet sand.

When I finished coughing and choking, I heard the voices.

Low voices. Nearby.

Low voices of men chanting in unison. . .

"The bones, they crack; the bones, they creep.
The men come alive in the briny deep.
You ended our death, you ended our sleep.
The men come alive in the briny deep."

"Nooooo." I heard Sheena moan beside me.

I tried to turn to her. But my face was sinking into the wet sand.

My brain whirred. I knew Captain Ben's dead pirates couldn't be here in HorrorLand. No way.

So how could we hear the same frightening chant? The same low voices?

I sucked in a deep breath and held it. The hot sand covered my nose. Everything went black as my head sank under the surface.

Can't see. Can't breathe.

And the chanting voices were all I could hear.

Down . . . down. . .

I held my breath till my lungs felt about to burst. My heart pounded in my chest.

Isn't anyone going to rescue us?

And then, with a loud *WHOOOOSH*, I was pulled down hard. The heavy sand fell away. I could breathe again. I could see, too. See that I was surrounded in darkness.

Faster. I was sliding on my back, straight down.

It took me a few seconds to realize I was in a narrow glass tube, smooth like a steep waterslide. I kept my arms pressed close to my sides as I shot down . . . harder . . . harder. . .

So hard and fast, and now it shot me *back up* again!

Wow! An awesome ride!

I sailed up high and burst through an opening back into bright sunlight. I could see the whole park down below. I saw the towers of the Stagger Inn . . . a tiny graveyard surrounded by woods . . . the bobbing black balloons in Zombie Plaza. . .

This is like flying, I thought.

And then I let out a cry as I was pulled down into the tube again. I slid back into a cold darkness.

A heartbeat later, strong hands grabbed my ankles. A grinning Horror pulled me out of the chute and set me on hard, solid ground.

My legs felt shaky. My heart was still racing.

The Horror raised an air blower – like a big electric hairdryer – and blew all the sand off me.

Two seconds later, Sheena came shooting out. Her hair stuck out wild around her head, as if she'd been struck by lightning. She had a huge grin on her face.

"Awesome!" she shouted, pumping her fist in the air. "First, it's terrifying. Then . . . *awesome!*"

The Horror blew the sand off her. Then we both started laughing and dancing around. It was such an *insane* thing to be sinking in sand and then flying in the sky!

"Hey—" After a few seconds, I stopped my crazy dance. I turned back to the chutes. "Where are Britney and Molly?"

Smoothing her hair down with both hands, Sheena stepped over to me. We both stared at the bottoms of the slides.

"Oh, no! They went under the same time we did!" I cried.

"So where *are* they?" Sheena asked.

I had a sudden heavy feeling in my stomach.

"Something's gone terribly wrong," I said. "They must be trapped under the quicksand!"

I ran to the Horror. He was sitting on a low stool, hunched over a copy of *Scary People* magazine.

"Did you see our friends?" I cried.

The Horror shook his head. He didn't look up from the magazine.

"But – but—" I sputtered. "They were with us. They sank in the quicksand with us."

"Didn't see them," the Horror muttered. He flicked a bee off his purple sleeve and it fluttered to the ground.

"But . . . they *had* to come out here, right?" I asked. "They couldn't disappear into thin air!"

He turned a page of the magazine. Finally, he looked up at me. "Beats me, kid," he said. "I only work here."

"But – but—" I stammered again.

He got a lopsided grin on his face. "Why don't you try Lost and Found?" he said. He chuckled to himself and lowered his face to the magazine.

"Big help," I muttered. I hurried back to Sheena. She was still staring at the slide.

"It's *got* to be just another HorrorLand scare," she said. "They both probably slid out somewhere else. That dude is just trying to scare us."

I glanced all around Quicksand Beach. No sign of the two girls. "Maybe you're right," I said. "Maybe they're waiting for us at the exit."

I turned and began to lead the way out. But I stopped when I heard a low voice. A raspy voice, faint but clear – so close to my ear, it gave me a chill:

"Ahoy, mate! Do ye want to see your friends again?"

I turned to Sheena. "Did you hear that?"

Her eyes were bulging, and her mouth had dropped open. "Captain Ben?" she whispered.

Impossible.

We both knew it was impossible.

I whirled around in a circle. No one in sight. Where did the voice come from? And the pirates chanting, too? Were there hidden speakers in the sand?

Sheena shuddered. "Someone here knows what happened to us this summer," she said in a trembling voice. "Someone is trying to scare us for *real*!"

We started to run. We had to get away from there.

I kept expecting to hear Captain Ben again. Or the frightening chants of his men.

Britney and Molly weren't waiting for us at the exit. We gazed up and down Quicksand Beach. Four or five kids were sinking in the sand, laughing as they struggled to climb out.

I led the way on to Zombie Plaza. I shielded my eyes from the bright sunlight and searched for the two girls. No sign of them.

"Weird," Sheena muttered. "Maybe they're back at the hotel?"

"Maybe," I said. I didn't know what to believe.

A Horror in a black apron stood behind a little green-and-purple cart. She held up a sugar cone. "You two look like you could use some ice cream," she said.

She was right. My throat was dry. I had hot beads of sweat running down my forehead. "What flavours do you have?" I asked.

She opened the lid and peered into the cart. "I've got Liver 'N' Onions," she said. "That's my most popular. And . . . let me see . . . I've still got some Calf's Brain Cookie Dough left."

Yuck. "Do you have vanilla?" I asked.

She nodded. "Yes. I have Vanilla Split Pea Onion Dip."

"No thanks," I said.

Sheena grinned at me. "Dare you to try the liver."

"No way," I said. I started to walk away. But she blocked the way. "Thought you're totally brave now. Go ahead. Try it."

The Horror scooped a big ball of ice cream on to the top of a cone. She handed it to me. "Liver on a garlic cone!"

My stomach gurgled. The ice cream was a *sick* green-brown. I saw big lumps in it.

"Hold your nose while you swallow it," the Horror said. "It helps a little."

My hand trembled. I held the cone away from me. But Sheena pushed it up to my face. "Go ahead, Billy, lick it. Be brave. Take a lick."

I held my breath. Then I stuck my tongue out and took a tiny lick. Ohhhhh. My stomach gurgled again.

"Hey!" I took another lick. Tasted it. Swallowed.

Then I burst out laughing. "It's chocolate!"

The Horror began to laugh, too. "Welcome to HorrorLand," she said.

Sheena and I shared the cone. Then we started to the hotel to find Britney and Molly.

I saw a banner strung across the plaza: THE PLAY PEN!

"That's the games arcade," I said. "You know. All those carnival games. It's on the way. Let's check it out."

"But what about the two girls?" Sheena asked.

"They'll be at the hotel. For sure," I said. "I just want to see what games they have here."

A sign over the gate read: IT'S NOT WHETHER YOU WIN OR LOSE — BUT HOW MUCH YOU SCREAM YOUR HEAD OFF!

I saw two long rows of game booths with a wide aisle in between. The aisle was jammed with people eager to play. They all seemed to be having a lot of fun.

"These games look awesome," I said. "Check that one out."

TARANTULA RACES.

We jogged closer. Four kids lined up in front of the booth. A Horror placed a live tarantula on each kid's head. "Don't let it fall off," the Horror said. "Last kid to get *bitten* wins!"

Sheena rolled her eyes. "Not my idea of a fun time," she said.

"We have a WINNER!" a Horror shouted from a game booth down the aisle. "You win a live RATTLESNAKE!" People laughed and cheered.

Across the aisle stood a game called HEAD TOSS. Two girls held real-looking human heads in their hands. The idea was to toss the head on to a tall metal spike. If it stuck on the spike, you won a prize.

We watched them toss their heads one at a time. The heads bounced off the spikes and rolled away. The girls walked off, shrugging their shoulders.

A boy about our age stepped up to the booth. The Horror handed him a head with short blond hair.

"Do we know that boy? He looks familiar," Sheena said. She pulled me closer.

The kid was tall and athletic-looking. He had wavy brown hair and brown eyes. He had a sleeveless black T-shirt pulled down over faded jeans.

I sniggered. "You just think he's cute."

"He *is* cute," Sheena said. "Look. Is he smiling at me? He has a great smile."

"He isn't smiling at you. The ugly head is smiling at you!" I said. "Why don't you go give it a big kiss?"

Sheena slapped my arm. "How funny are *you*? Not!"

The boy raised the head in one hand. But before he tossed it, he reached into his jeans pocket. I thought he was reaching for a token. The games all required copper-coloured HorrorLand tokens.

But no. He pulled out a small grey card. He tapped the card twice on the side of the booth.

"What's *that* about?" I whispered.

Sheena shrugged. "Maybe it's some kind of good-luck charm," she said.

The boy tossed the head. It slid on to a spike, spun a few times – and stayed on.

"A winner!" the Horror shouted. "Hey, every-body – we have a winner!"

Sheena and I followed the boy down the row of carnival booths. He stopped at one with a red sign: SPIN THE WHEEL OF MISFORTUNE!

The big wheel was covered with bad things that could happen to a person – Headache, Itchy Where You Can't Scratch, Spider on Your Tongue, Beheading. . . Only two squares on the wheel read: WINNER.

"No way he can win this one," I muttered. "Why does he even want to try it? You can only lose."

The kid stepped up to the wheel. But again, he didn't put in a token. Instead, he pulled out that grey card. He tapped it twice on the side of the booth. Then he slid it back in his pocket.

He spun the wheel hard. *Click click click.* It went around and around for at least a minute. And it stopped on WINNER.

The Horror scratched his head. "I don't believe it," he murmured. "Our first winner!"

"This dude can't lose!" I said to Sheena.

"And did I mention he's *cute*, too?" she said, grinning.

We followed him to a game called Vampire Darts. The sign read: SEND A SILVER DART INTO THE VAMPIRE'S HEART!

The Horror handed the kid a long silver dart. The target was a tiny red heart on the back wall of the booth.

The kid tapped the little grey card twice on the side of the booth. Then he aimed and tossed the dart.

And three guesses what happened. Yes. Winner again!

"This is too good to be true!" I said.

And maybe it was. Because everything changed all at once.

The Horror in the dart booth didn't hand him a prize. Instead, he signalled to two Horrors across the aisle. The Horrors wore black and orange Monster Police uniforms with big silver badges on their chests. They turned instantly and began moving towards him.

The boy took off running.

"Stop right there!" one of the Horrors shouted. "Stop – *now*!"

They pushed past a group of kids and hurtled after the boy.

The boy ran towards us. His brown hair was flying up behind him. I could see the look of panic on his face.

"Hey!" I cried out as he bumped up against me.

He shoved something into my hand. "Hide it," he gasped. "Quick. Hide it."

He didn't stop. He zigzagged through the crowd, down the long carnival aisle.

The two Monster Police tramped past Sheena and me, running hard. People screamed and jumped out of their way.

I opened my hand and studied the object the boy gave me. It was a grey plastic card. A room key card. I shoved it into my jeans pocket and kept my hand around it.

"Oh, no!" Sheena cried out as the two Monster Police caught up to the boy. One held him. The other one searched his pockets.

"This is *sick*! What do they *want*?" Sheena cried.

I knew what they were searching for – the key card.

But why? What was the big deal about a plastic card?

"Uh-oh." I gasped. One of the two cops suddenly turned. He narrowed his eyes at Sheena and me.

Did he see the boy hand the card to me?

The cop started towards me, moving fast. His partner let go of the boy and followed.

"They're coming over here!" Sheena cried. "What do they want? What should we *do*?"

Sheena and I pushed through a group of teenagers in front of the darts booth. Then we lowered our heads – and *ran*.

I jumped over a baby pushchair – ignored the startled cries of the mom and dad – and kept going.

"Whoa!" I skidded to a stop in front of a ten-foot-tall gorilla. A man in a costume? I didn't wait around to figure it out. The gorilla let out a roar. I squeezed right through his legs and took off.

Our trainers pounded on the concrete. Sheena and I darted across Zombie Plaza. I kept glancing back. No sign of the two Monster Police. Did they lose us in the crowd?

Gasping for breath, I slipped into the hotel. I held the door for Sheena. We ran through the lobby, into the lift.

We didn't say a word till we reached my room.

Then we both collapsed on to the long sofa, panting, groaning, wiping sweat off our foreheads.

"Oh, wow," Sheena muttered. "Oh, wow. Oh, wow. What was *that* about?"

"They were looking for this," I said. I reached into my pocket and pulled out the plastic card. "That boy – he gave it to me when he ran past."

"What is it?" Sheena grabbed it from my hand and studied it. "The card he kept tapping on the booths. Weird. Look – it has words on it."

She handed it back. I turned it over in my hand. "The letter P," I said. "The rest has all been rubbed off."

Sheena scrunched up her face. "P? What does it stand for? Play Pen? The name of the game arcade?"

"Beats me." I shoved it into my pocket. "He told me to hide it."

Sheena's mouth dropped open. "Billy – we forgot about Britney and Molly! How *could* we?" she cried. "I . . . I hope they came back to the hotel."

I picked up the room phone. "I'll call the hotel operator," I said. "See if I can get their room."

"I'm really worried," Sheena said, hugging herself. "I hope they're OK."

"Me, too," I said. I pushed 0 and waited for the operator to come on.

I heard two rings. Then a click. Then. . .

"HAHAHAHAHAHAHAHAHA!"

I pulled the phone away from my ear. "It's just a man laughing," I told Sheena. "Listen."

I shoved the phone to her ear.

"HAHAHAHAHAHAHAHAHA!"

"What a totally nasty, evil laugh!" Sheena exclaimed. She slammed the receiver down. Then she picked it up again. "Let's try another number."

She pushed the number for room service.

"HAHAHAHAHAHAHAHAHA!"

I felt a chill run down my back. "Do you remember that laugh?" I asked.

Sheena gasped. "It sounds like Captain Ben!"

She pushed 0 again, and we both listened.

"HAHAHAHAHAHAHAHAHA!"

The phone fell out of Sheena's hand. She started to tremble. She grabbed my arm. "Billy," she whispered, "let's get *out* of here!"

We stepped out into the long, dark hall. I pulled the door shut behind us. The evil laughter still rang in my ears. Every time I heard it, I felt cold all over.

"Where are we going?" I asked.

"To the front desk," Sheena said. "We've got to find out about Britney and Molly before we leave."

We made our way quickly down the hall. The lift doors creaked open – and a boy stepped out. The boy who gave me the weird key card.

"Hey—" He let out a startled cry. "You guys again! You're on the thirteenth floor, too?"

"They let you go!" I cried.

"That was totally *disturbing*!" he said. "Do you *believe* that? What was their *problem*?"

He said his name was Matt Daniels. I handed him back his card. "Why did those Monster Police want it so badly?" I asked.

"No clue," he said. He turned to Sheena. "Sorry if I got you two in trouble."

"No problem," Sheena said. Her cheeks turned pink. She really *did* have a crush on him. "Where'd you get that card?"

Matt held it in front of him. "It was way weird. A Horror came up to me on the Plaza. He shoved it into my hand. He looked really nervous. He said to guard it. He said it would take me places."

I squinted at it. "Take you *where*?"

Matt shrugged. "Beats me. The Horror took off before I could ask him anything. I tried using it on those games. I think it helped me win – and I didn't even need tokens."

"That is totally disturbing," I said.

Matt tucked the card into his pocket. "I didn't want to give it to those cops. The Horror told me to guard it. And . . . I want to see what else it can do."

"We're going to the front desk," Sheena told him. "Two girls we met, Britney and Molly. . . They went with us to Quicksand Beach. But they didn't come out. We want to see if they came back here."

She flashed Matt a smile. "Want to come with us?"

Matt shrugged. "Sure," he said.

Creaking and groaning, the lift carried us down to the first floor. "My room is awesome," Matt said as we waited for the doors to open. "And it's free.

Believe that? I got some kind of free invitation. I don't know why."

"So did we," I said. "It's like a big mystery. How did we get picked?"

"Britney and Molly, too," Sheena said. "I guess we won some kind of contest. But Billy and I don't remember entering any contest."

"Me either," Matt muttered. "Weird."

On the first floor, we stepped out into a long hall. The walls were covered in fake cobwebs. And giant spiders bobbed and spun from webs dangling from the ceiling lights.

We passed a row of rooms, then turned a corner. "I think the front desk is that way," I said, pointing.

But Sheena and Matt weren't listening to me. They were staring into a wide glass window. I saw the word CAFÉ in big red letters on a sign above the window.

"Oh, wow!" Sheena cried. She pulled me to the window.

I peered into the café. "It's Britney and Molly!" I cried.

The two girls sat across from each other. They were at a little round table in front of a huge mirror that hung on the wall. They had tall ice cream sodas in front of them. But neither girl had taken a sip.

"Why do they look so sad?" I asked.

Sheena pounded on the glass and shouted, "Hey – Britney! Molly!"

The two girls stared at each other. They didn't move.

Sheena pounded harder on the window. "They can't hear us," she said. "Let's go in."

I grabbed the door and tried to pull it open. It didn't budge. I tried pushing it. No way. I shoved harder. No.

I pressed my face against the glass to get a better look inside. No other entrance. No other windows.

"Why can't they hear us?" Sheena cried. She pounded on the window with her fists. She cupped her hands around her mouth and screamed their names.

The two girls didn't move.

I pounded on the door. Then I kicked the door. It made a thunderous *BANG*.

The girls sat staring at their ice cream sodas.

"What's going on?" I cried. "Why can't they hear us?"

Sheena didn't give up. My sister *never* gives up. She pounded on the window and shouted their names.

"What's *that*?" Matt asked. He pointed to a metal box next to the door. "Check it out. It has a slot in it. Maybe our room keys open the door."

I pulled my purple and green key card from my wallet. I shoved it into the slot and tried the door. No. It didn't budge.

I had an idea. "Matt," I said. "Try the secret card. Maybe you need that weird card to get into this restaurant."

"Worth a try," Matt said. He pushed the grey card into the slot.

A green light flashed on. The door buzzed. He pushed it open. "Yes!" he cried. "We're in! We—"

I followed him into the café – and stopped short. I let out a startled cry. "Hey!"

We were standing in an empty room.

136

"Where'd they go?" I cried.

"The place is totally empty!" Matt said.

I walked over to Britney and Molly's table. No ice cream sodas. The napkins were neatly folded. The cutlery hadn't been used.

"Weird," I muttered. I turned and gazed into the mirror. It covered the entire back wall. My reflection and Matt's reflection stared back at us.

One reflection was missing.

"Sheena?" I called. "Where are you? Where did you go?"

"Don't be funny," Sheena said. "I'm standing right next to you."

I spun around. My breath caught in my throat. "But . . . I can't see you!" I cried.

"Don't be stupid," Sheena said. "This is no time for dumb jokes."

"I can't see you, either, Sheena," Matt said. "It's not a joke. Look." He pointed to the mirror.

I turned and looked again. And saw the two of us in the mirror. My reflection stood next to Matt's reflection.

Beside me, I heard Sheena gasp. "Oh – *no*. I . . . I'm INVISIBLE!"

To be continued in . . .

③ MONSTER BLOOD FOR BREAKFAST!

But first . . .

Before HorrorLand,
Billy and Sheena starred in

DEEP TROUBLE

Turn the page for a peek at
R.L. Stine's classic prequel.

"Help!" I cried out again. "Sheena! Dr D!"

I was dragged below the surface again. I felt the slimy tentacle tighten around my ankle.

As I sank underwater, I turned – and saw it.

It loomed huge and dark.

A sea monster!

Through the churning waters, it glared at me with one giant brown eye. The terrifying creature floated underwater like an enormous, dark green balloon. Its mouth opened in a silent cry, revealing two rows of jagged, sharp teeth.

An enormous octopus! But it had at least *twelve* tentacles!

Twelve long, slimy tentacles. One was wrapped around my ankle. Another one slid towards me.

NO!

My arms thrashed the water.

I gulped in mouthfuls of air.

I struggled to the surface – but the huge creature dragged me down again.

I couldn't believe it. As I sank, scenes from my life actually flashed before my eyes.

I saw my parents, waving to me as I boarded the yellow school bus for my first day of school.

Mom and Dad! I'll never see them again!

What a way to go, I thought. Killed by a sea monster!

No one will believe it.

Everything started to turn red. I felt dizzy, weak.

But something was pulling me, pulling me up.

Up to the surface. Away from the tentacled monster.

I opened my eyes, choking and sputtering.

I stared up at Dr D!

"Billy! Are you all right?" Dr D studied me with concern.

I coughed and nodded. I kicked my right leg. The slimy tentacle was gone.

The dark creature had vanished.

"I heard you screaming and saw you thrashing about," said Dr D. "I swam over from the boat as fast as I could. What happened?"

Dr D had a yellow life jacket over his shoulders. He slipped a rubber lifesaver ring over my head. I floated easily now, the life ring under my arms.

I had lost my flippers in the struggle. My mask and snorkel dangled around my neck.

Sheena swam over and floated beside me, treading water.

"It grabbed my leg!" I cried breathlessly. "It tried to pull me under!"

"What grabbed your leg, Billy?" asked Dr D. "I don't see anything around here—"

"It was a sea monster," I told him. "A huge one! I felt its slimy tentacle grabbing my leg. . . *Ouch!*"

Something pinched my toe.

"It's back!" I shrieked in horror.

Sheena popped out of the water and shook her wet hair, laughing.

"That was me, you dork!" she cried.

"Billy, Billy," Dr D murmured. "You and your wild imagination." He shook his head. "You nearly scared me to death. Please – don't ever do that again. Your leg probably got tangled in a piece of seaweed, that's all."

"But – but—!" I sputtered.

He dipped his hand in the water and pulled up a handful of slimy green strings. "There's seaweed everywhere."

"But I saw it!" I shouted. "I saw its tentacles, its big, pointy teeth!"

"There's no such thing as sea monsters," said Sheena. Miss Know-It-All.

"Let's discuss it on the boat," my uncle said, dropping the clump of seaweed back in the water.

"Come on. Swim back with me. And stay away from the reef. Swim around it."

He turned around and started swimming towards the *Cassandra*. I saw that the sea monster had pulled me into the lagoon. The reef lay between us and the boat. But there was a break in the reef we could swim through.

I followed them, thinking angry thoughts.

Why didn't they believe me?

I had seen the creature grab my leg. It wasn't a stupid clump of seaweed. It wasn't my imagination.

I was determined to prove them wrong. I'd find that creature and show it to them myself – someday. But not today.

Now I was ready to get back to the safety of the boat.

I swam up to Sheena and called, "Race you to the boat."

"Last one there is a chocolate-covered jellyfish!" she cried.

Sheena can't refuse a race. She started speeding towards the boat, but I caught her by the arm.

"Wait," I said. "No fair. You're wearing flippers. Take them off."

"Too bad!" she cried, and pulled away. "See you at the boat!" I watched her splash away, building a good lead.

She's not going to win, I decided.

I stared at the reef up ahead.

It would be faster just to swim over the reef. A short cut.

I turned and started to swim straight towards the red coral.

"Billy! Get back here!" Dr D shouted.

I pretended I didn't hear him.

The reef loomed ahead. I was almost there.

I saw Sheena splashing ahead of me. I kicked extra-hard. I knew she'd never have the guts to swim over the reef. She'd swim around the end of it. I would cut through and beat her.

But my arms suddenly began to ache. I wasn't used to swimming so far.

Maybe I can stop at the reef and rest my arms for a second, I thought.

I reached the reef. I turned around. Sheena was swimming to the left, around the reef. I figured I had a few seconds to rest.

I stepped on to the red coral reef –

– and screamed in horror!

About the Author

R.L. Stine's book are read all over the world. So far, his books have sold more than 300 million copies, making him one of the most popular children's authors in history. Besides Goosebumps, R.L. Stine has written the teen series Fear Street and the funny series Rotten School, as well as the Mostly Ghostly series, The Nightmare Room series, and the two-book thriller *Dangerous Girls*. R.L. Stine lives in New York with his wife, Jane, and Minnie, his King Charles spaniel. You can learn more about him at www.RLStine.com.

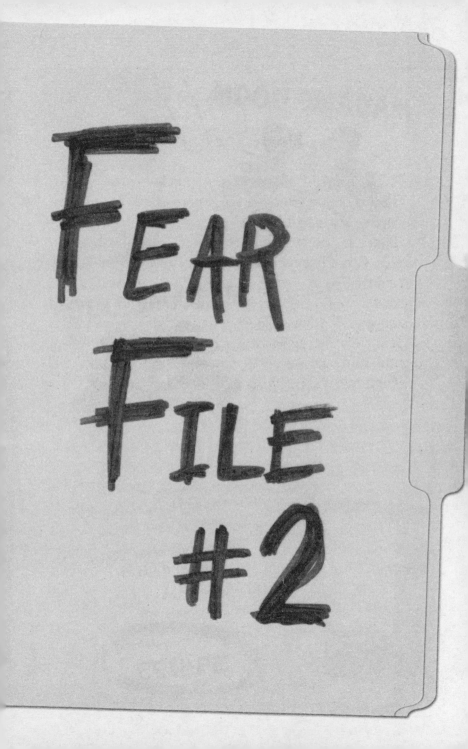

MADAME DOOM

MADAME DOOM

Stay away and leave the unlucky
ones to their fate.

This message is for **YOU,
Luke and Lizzy!**

Drop another token in the slot
and I will tell you more.

Your Lucky Numbers:

394)23

BLACK LAGOON
WATER PARK

Rules and Regulations

Quicksand Beach

- You must be at least 44 inches tall to sink.
- Do not scream or shout for help. You might disturb other sinkers.
- Animal skulls are NOT souvenirs.
- Be sure to visit the toilet BEFORE sinking.

Loch Ness Lake

- Do not believe rumours. There's no such thing as a man-eating squid.
- If you drink the water, don't swallow the brown, lumpy stuff.
- Lifeguards are no longer on duty due to rumours of a man-eating squid.

FIND THE REST at WWW.ESCAPEHorrorLAND.COM

SIGNED: LM1

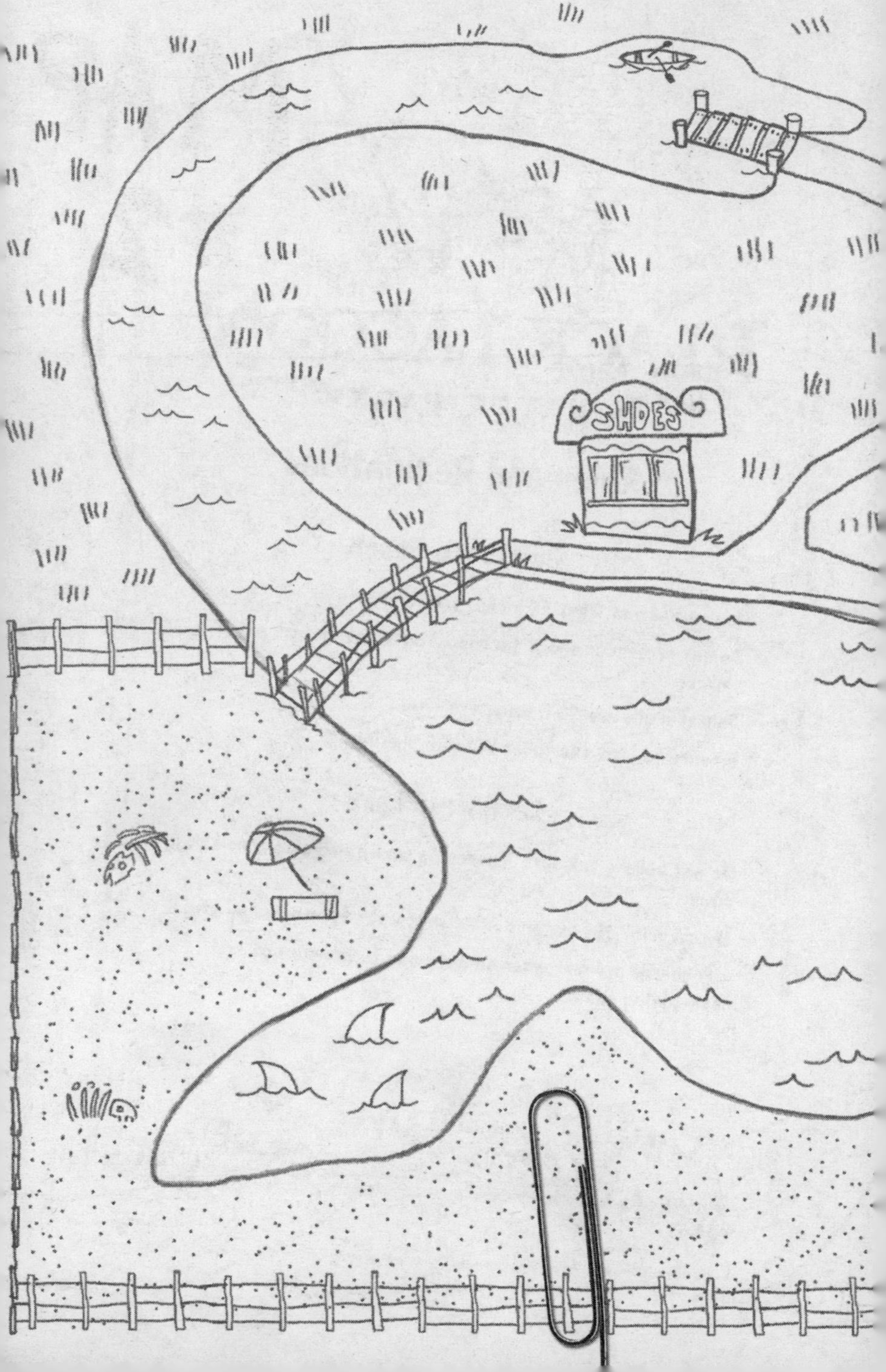
SHOES

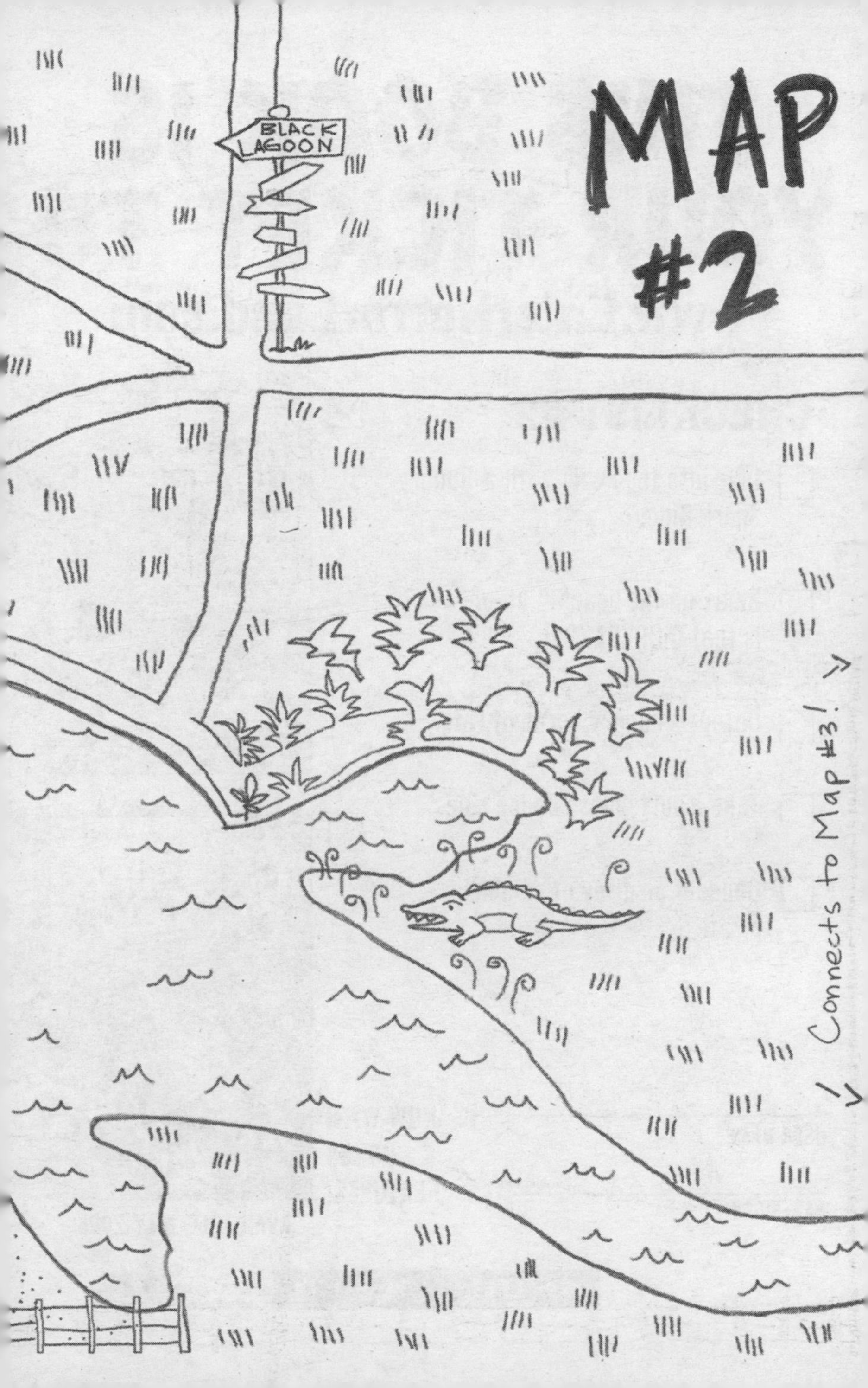
MAP #2
BLACK LAGOON
Connects to Map #3!

THIS BOOK IS YOUR TICKET TO

www.EnterHorrorLand.com

CHECKLIST #2

- [ ] Dive into the Swim-with-a-Hungry-Shark Ride.

- [ ] Relax on the beach…uh-oh, is that QUICKSAND?!

- [ ] Defeat a hungry horde of rats.

- [ ] Take a bottomless canoe ride.

- [ ] Conquer an army of zombie pirates!

NOW WITH BONUS FEATURES!

AVAILABLE JULY 2008

_____

USER NAME

_____

PASSWORD